THE TEXAS TATTLER

All the news that's barely fit to print!

Baby Bryan Fortune Kidnapped!

Town of Red Rock, Texas, shaken to its bedrock.

The cooing heir to the Fortune empire was snatched from his nursery in the sprawling Double Crown Ranch mansion last evening during the infant's christening celebration. Late breaking reports indicate that Matthew and Claudia Fortune, baby Bryan's parents, are frantic and eager for leads. The Texas governor pledges his support to one of the Lone Star State's richest families.

Red Rock's and San Antonio's finest are on the case, but inside sources reveal that their official "no comment" means "baffled and clueless." Is this heinous crime a desperate ploy for money...or revenge? Police are investigating all persons suspected of having a vendetta against the Fortune clan. Now, *that's* a long list....

And another enticing Fortune tidbit: Sources in the know reveal that infamous bachelor Holden Fortune must wed a respectable lady as a condition of inheriting a dime of dear old daddy's legacy. Is it a mere coincidence, then, that earlier this week the reputed playboy was spotted escorting Dr. Lucinda Brightwater—dressed in a stunning *white* suit—up the courthouse stairs? When questioned, Holden said he was "fixing a traffic ticket." For what? Excessive speeding...to the altar?!

D0981599

About the Author

MAGGIE SHAYNE

A national bestselling author whom *Romantic Times Magazine* calls "brilliantly inventive," Maggie has written more than fifteen novels for Silhouette Books.

She has also won numerous awards, including a *Romantic Times Magazine* Career Achievement Award, and is a three-time finalist for the Romance Writers of America's prestigious RITA Award. She also writes mainstream contemporary fantasy.

In her spare time, Maggie enjoys collecting gemstones, reading tarot cards, hanging out on the Genie computer network and spending time outdoors. She lives in a rural town in central New York with her husband, Rick, five beautiful daughters and a bulldog named Wrinkles.

Watch for Maggie Shayne's next release from Silhouette Books:
THE OUTLAW BRIDE
December 1999
Silhouette Intimate Moments

Maggie Shayne

MILLION DOLLAR MARRIAGE

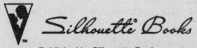

Published by Silhouette Books

America's Publisher of Contemporary Romance

Special thanks and acknowledgment are given to Maggie Shayne for her contribution to The Fortunes of Texas series.

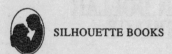

SILHOUETTE BOOKS

ISBN 0-373-65030-2

MILLION DOLLAR MARRIAGE

Visit us at www.romance.net

Printed in U.S.A.

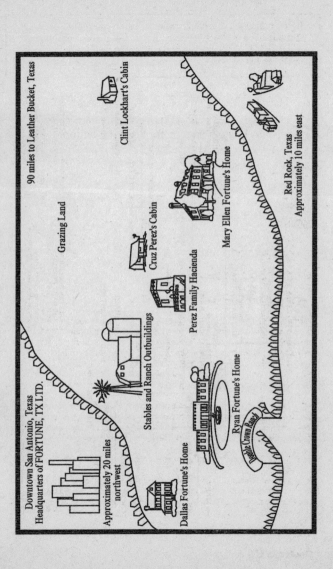

Downtown San Antonio, Texas
Headquarters of FORTUNE, TX LTD.

Approximately 20 miles
northwest

Dallas Fortune's Home

Stables and Ranch Outbuildings

Grazing Land

Cruz Perez's Cabin

Perez Family Hacienda

Ryan Fortune's Home

Mary Ellen Fortune's Home

Clint Lockhart's Cabin

90 miles to Leather Bucket, Texas

Red Rock, Texas
Approximately 10 miles east

Double Crown Ranch

THE FORTUNES OF TEXAS

KINGSTON FORTUNE (d)

1st marriage
PATIENCE TALBOT (d)
Teddy §

2nd marriage
SELENA HOBBS (d)

MIRANDA
m Lloyd Carter (D)

KANE **GABRIELLE** ⑧

RYAN

1st marriage
JANINE LOCKHART (d)

MATTHEW **ZANE** ⑫
m
Claudia Beaumont
Bryan

DALLAS ④
m
Sara Andersen (d)

VANESSA ② ***—***VICTORIA ⑩

2nd marriage
SOPHIA BARNES

CLINT LOCKHART
brother of
JACE LOCKHART ⑥

† **ROSITA** and **RUBEN PEREZ**

Anita Carmen Frieda **CRUZ** ③

MAGGIE ④
m
Craig Randall (D)
Travis

CAMERON (d)
m
MARY ELLEN LOCKHART

HOLDEN ① **LOGAN** ⑤ **EDEN** ⑦
Sawyer*

LILY REDGROVE
m
Chester Cassidy (d)

COLE* ⑪ **HANNAH** ⑨ **MARIA**
James a.k.a. Taylor

---

* Child of affair
d Deceased
D Divorced
m. Married
*** Twins
— Affair
† Loyal ranch staff
§ Kidnapped by maternal grandfather

TITLES:

1. MILLION DOLLAR MARRIAGE
2. THE BABY PURSUIT
3. EXPECTING...IN TEXAS
4. A WILLING WIFE
5. CORPORATE DADDY
6. SNOWBOUND CINDERELLA
7. THE SHEIKH'S SECRET SON
8. THE HEIRESS AND THE SHERIFF
9. LONE STAR WEDDING
10. IN THE ARMS OF A HERO
11. WEDLOCKED?!
12. HIRED BRIDE

THE FORTUNES OF TEXAS™

 Meet the Fortunes of Texas

Holden Fortune: The high-powered executive doesn't want to settle down. But he would do anything to secure his inheritance, including proposing marriage to a beautiful baby doctor....

Lucinda Brightwater: The lovely lady's biological clock is ticking louder with each bundle of joy she delivers. She can think of only one way to make her own baby dream come true—seduce her convenient husband....

Ryan Fortune: Beloved patriarch of the Fortune family of Texas. When fate brings his lost love back into his life, Ryan vows not to let anything stop him from claiming Lily Cassidy as his bride...not even what proves to be the most scandalous divorce of the decade.

Vanessa Fortune: When her precious nephew is kidnapped, she is determined to help with the search. Will she be able to reunite baby Bryan with his parents, and can her own romance be far away...?

Prologue

Red Rock High School
Valentine's Day Dance, 1983

Holden Fortune was the man of her dreams. But he'd never give a girl like her a second glance. Lucinda Brightwater sat in a chair near the wall where it was dim and shadowy. She didn't usually come to school dances. She didn't know why she'd bothered coming to this one, unless it was just to torture herself, which was precisely what she was doing.

He was dancing now, his current girlfriend, Tiffany Lambert, wrapped tight in his arms as he moved her slowly around the floor. The glittering globe overhead reflected flashes of light on his honey-blond hair. He was so handsome, so athletic, so popular—easily the most popular boy in school, and that was only partially because he came from one of the richest families in Texas. Lucinda had loved him since fifth grade. But he'd barely noticed her.

She was plain. Her straight, dark hair wouldn't do anything but hang there, no matter how she cut or sprayed or styled it. She wasn't allowed to wear more than a hint of makeup, and if she'd tried dressing in the half tops and short skirts that were popular with the "in crowd," her father would have gone into cardiac arrest. Besides all that, she was too smart. All brains and no beauty. A nerd. A geek.

Tiffany, on the other hand, was bleached to a sun-shiny shade of blond and her hair was always perfect. Layers on the sides, fluffed up high on the top. Her skirts were short and flouncy, and she probably didn't even own a shirt that came down as far as her navel. She wore several bracelets on each arm, huge gold earrings that shook when she moved, and enough makeup to sink a small ship. She knew how to send sidelong glances Holden's way, how to giggle, how to flirt. All the things Lucinda had never been any good at. Oh, Tiffany was failing most of her classes, but Holden didn't seem to care much about her grades. Lucinda knew perfectly well that Tiffany was well ed-ucated in...other areas. She was not an inexperienced virgin like Lucinda.

The music died down, and the couples on the floor parted and moved toward the sides of the decorated school gym, or toward the punch bowl, or sneaked off toward the exits hoping for a chance to slip outside, unseen by the chaperones.

Holden and Tiffany, however, stayed where they were. She was looking up at him, speaking very quickly, and then he was saying something back to her. He looked upset. Tiffany shook her head hard, side to side, earrings jangling. She turned away. Hol-den gripped her arm to pull her back, and she hauled off and slapped him. Hard.

Lucinda sucked in a loud gasp, jumping to her feet, a reflex action she didn't even think about first. Tif-fany stormed away from poor Holden without a back-ward glance, and Holden, looking wounded and shocked, stared after her. Then, a moment later, he seemed to shake himself. Turning away, he wandered off in the opposite direction, and vanished into a crowd.

Lucinda just stood there for a long time, hoping he'd emerge again. She was going to go over to him, ask him if he was okay. She would. She'd just drum up all of her courage and talk to him. She couldn't believe Tiffany would break up with him that way, in front of half the school. No girl in her right mind would treat a guy like Holden that way. Lucinda certainly wouldn't. If he were hers... She sighed and closed her eyes. Who was she kidding? It would never happen. Guys like Holden didn't date girls like Lucinda. She might as well accept that and forget about him. In a few months he'd graduate, head off to college, and she'd probably never see him again.

Holden was good and pissed. It wasn't enough that Tiffany Lambert had to be the first girl in history to ever dump him before he got around to dumping her, but she had to do it in front of everyone. And she'd slapped him!

He was furious when he stalked off into a corner, but the guys quickly surrounded him, slapping his shoulder and saying things like, "Who needs her anyway?" and "Hell, Holden, you can have any girl you want. What do you care?"

He agreed with all those sentiments, of course. And the liquor helped. Billy Martin had smuggled a bottle of Seagram's into the gym, and he opened his coat to give Holden a peek. Holden nodded, and then they all sauntered off to the boys' bathroom and passed the bottle around.

The more Holden drank, the angrier he got. And by the time he and the other boys staggered back into the gym, carefully avoiding any sharp-eyed chaperones, he was feeling the need for vengeance. Tiffany was standing in the corner talking to a bunch of her friends, most of whom Holden had slept with. He decided to make her jealous, remind her she wasn't the only girl on the planet.

He scanned the chairs that lined the gym walls for a suitable dance partner, and then froze when his gaze fell on pretty little Lucinda Brightwater. His throat went dry. He licked his lips. Lucinda was…different. Quiet. Shy. Very deep and very intelligent. She wasn't the kind of girl a guy like Holden should get himself involved with. She was not a giggling teen out for a good time. She was a lady. She reminded Holden a lot of his own mother, with her quiet grace and soft-spoken dignity.

And he reminded himself of his father. How many times had his dad told him how alike they were? Called him a chip off the old block? They even looked alike. And Cameron changed mistresses almost monthly, while Mary Ellen, Holden's mother, some-how managed to forgive him every time. She was the saddest person Holden knew.

No. He didn't belong with girls like Lucinda Bright-water. Nice girls. Sweet girls. Girls who would let him break their fragile hearts. He had convinced himself of that a long time ago. He'd stick to shallow, loose girls out for a good time, girls who wouldn't take things too seriously. Girls who wouldn't get hurt. Like Tiffany Lambert.

But tonight, he was drunk. And he was stinging from that slap and the public humiliation that went with it. And he was itching to show Tiffany that he didn't need her, that he could have a real lady. One Tiffany could never measure up to. A flawless white rose of a girl almost too good to be touched.

Holden sucked in a breath, and managed to walk without staggering over to where Lucinda sat. Her raven hair hung over her shoulders, straight and gleaming. Dark eyes widened at his approach, and rose to stare into his. And her copper-toned skin seemed as smooth as satin.

"Would you dance with me, Lucy?" he asked. So far as he knew, no one ever called her Lucy. He thought of her that way, though. Secretly, he thought of her as Lucinda in the Sky. The only girl he knew who was completely beyond his reach, out of his league.

She nodded slowly, eyes dark and mysterious. Getting to her feet, she stepped closer to him. Holden put his arms around her waist and pulled her toward him. Not quite touching, not yet. Even with as much as he'd had to drink, he didn't forget that she was a lady. Her hands linked together at the base of Holden's neck, and she moved her feet with his.

"Are you all right?" she asked him.

He looked down at her, nodded once. "You saw what happened, huh?"

"Everyone did." She bit her lower lip. "Sorry."

"Don't be. Tiffany's not." He stumbled a little and pulled Lucy closer. Expecting her to pull away at once, Holden was a little surprised when instead, she hesitated, then lowered her head to his shoulder.

Her hair smelled good. He slid his arms more completely around her waist.

"So, is that why you're dancing with me, Holden?" she asked softly. "To make Tiffany jealous?"

He frowned down at her, then stumbled again, would have fallen if she hadn't held him, steadied him.

"You're drunk, aren't you?" Leaning up so close he thought she was going to kiss him, she sniffed instead. "You are. I can smell it on you. I should have known." Taking herself out of his arms, she turned to walk away.

But then she stopped and faced him again. "You brought your car, didn't you? The one your father gave you for your eighteenth birthday?"

He smiled slowly. So she wanted to ride in his Vette, did she? Somehow he hadn't thought the car would hold the same appeal to a girl like Lucy that it did to the party girls he usually dated. But he was suddenly very glad. "Sure I did," he said.

Lucy sighed, shaking her head. "There's no way you can drive home. Come on. I'll take you in my mom's car, and you can come back for yours in the morning. Sober."

Holden frowned, totally confused. "You don't want to ride in the Vette?"

"I could care less about the Vette. I would feel pretty bad, though, if I got up in the morning and heard that you'd wrapped it around a pole and got yourself killed."

"You would, huh?"

She looked away from him, and when she looked

back her eyes were wider. "Crabtree is coming over here. Act sober for heaven's sake!"

Holden plastered his most sober expression on his face, folded his arms and leaned back, thinking the wall would support him. Only there was nothing to lean back on, so he fell flat on his ass.

Ms. Crabtree glared down at him. "Have you been drinking again, Mr. Fortune?" Her hands went to her hips and she tapped her foot.

"Drinking? Who, me? No way...I wouldn't even—"

"I can smell it from here, young man." Ms. Crabtree shook her head. "I guess I'm going to have to call your father to come and get you. He won't be amused by this latest example of your reckless behavior, Holden."

"Ms. Crabtree, it isn't Holden's fault," Lucy said quickly.

Crabtree looked at her, then frowned hard. No teacher in the history of the world had ever doubted a word Lucinda Brightwater said. They all seemed to think she was some kind of angel. She kept talking, and Holden thought maybe he agreed with them.

"Someone spiked the punch," she went on. "Holden didn't know about it until he'd already had several glasses."

Crabtree's face went from cold to wary. "Are you sure about this, Lucinda?"

"Positive. I—I heard someone talking about it in the girls' room."

"Who?"

"I don't know. I didn't see who, and it wasn't a voice I knew."

Crabtree eyed the punch bowl, and her look changed again, to one of alarm. "Oh, my."

"I didn't have any of the punch, Ms. Crabtree," Lucy went on. "And I'll drive Holden home. There's no need to call his father. He'd only blame you and the school for this anyway."

The teacher looked up sharply, as if she hadn't thought of that before, and then seemed thoughtful. "Are you sure you didn't have any of the punch, dear?"

"I wouldn't think of driving if I had, Ms. Crabtree," she said, sounding like a saint.

"Of course you wouldn't. All right, then. Get him home, and I'll dump the punch down the drain and make a fresh batch." She walked away muttering that she'd have to check every single student who planned to drive tonight before letting them leave.

Holden was still sitting on the gym floor. When Lucy reached down to help him up, he took her hand and let her, giving her a crooked smile. "I owe you one, Lucinda in the Sky."

"Yeah," she said. "You do."

She felt so nervous she could barely keep her mom's car on the road as she drove Holden toward his home. He wouldn't invite her inside. She knew he wouldn't. She would die if he did. But he wouldn't.

The place was a mansion. Tall and stately. So elegant with its pristine white paint, gleaming black shutters, and two-story porch spanning the entire front of the place, its columns stretching from top to bottom. It was almost...presidential. In a very Texas kind of way.

She pulled into the paved, curving driveway. No lights glowed from inside the house, only outdoor lights shone. Twin rows of them, lining either side of the sidewalk from driveway to front porch. And more, gleaming from around back.

"Come in for a minute?" Holden asked.

Oh, God, he *did* ask. His voice was slurred and she knew better than to accept. She really did.

"Okay," she said. She got out of the car and Holden took her arm. She wasn't sure if he took it because he wanted to touch her, or because he needed to hold on for balance. But either way, they walked together up the sidewalk, toward the porch and the front door.

"Holden, your parents... Don't you think you ought to go in the back way or something? If they see you like this..."

"They're out," he told her. "See? Dad's Caddy isn't here. There was some charity thing. Won't be home for hours. And the kids—Logan and Eden—are spending the night at Uncle Ryan's."

"Oh." Her throat was suddenly dry.

Holden led her across the wide porch, dug for a key under the doormat, and unlocked the massive doors. They were double, with stained-glass insets in a fan pattern, and complemented on either side by rectangular glass windows as tall as the doors themselves.

Opening one of the doors, Holden pulled her inside. "See? I told you." He looked around the dark foyer, shrugged. "No one's here. Come on."

"Wh-where are we going?"

"My room."

"I don't think that's a very good idea," she said.

Holden smiled in the darkness, and reached for a light switch. "Fine. The living room?"

When he flicked the lights on, things seemed less frightening to her.

"That would be better." She relaxed and followed Holden along the massive foyer and through a wide, arching doorway into the living room. He promptly collapsed on a huge leather sofa that smelled so rich she couldn't believe it. She sat down carefully beside him.

"I see you around school a lot," he said, leaning his head back on the sofa, closing his eyes. "At football practice, or in the cafeteria. In the halls sometimes. Near my locker."

She shrugged, and felt her face heat.

"You like me, don't you, Lucy?"

When she didn't answer, he opened his eyes, sat up a little.

"Don't look so surprised. What, did you think I hadn't noticed?"

"You never seem to notice me," she replied, then bit her lip.

"God, you're so stiff. Sit back, Lucy. Relax a little."

Taking a deep breath, she leaned back, only to find his arm now encircled her shoulders. "It's okay, you know. I like you, too. Always have."

"You...you do?"

He smiled crookedly. And the next thing she knew he was turning her toward him, bending close, and kissing her. His kiss was wet and insistent; his tongue sloppy when he began sliding it in and out of her mouth. Was this the way it was supposed to be? He tasted like whatever sort of liquor he'd been drinking. Smelled like it, too. And within a moment, his hand was under her sweater, inside her bra, closing over her breast.

She pushed him away. "Holden...stop."

Sitting up, blinking down at her, he stared for a long time. Then he shook his head. "Sorry. I...don't know what I was thinking. You're not that kind of girl." He pressed a hand to his forehead as if trying to squeeze some sense into it. "I know better than to act like that with you."

It was, she realized, her moment of truth. One of the most defining moments of her life. She was seventeen years old, and a virgin. And here was her chance to change that...with the only boy she would ever want in that way. The one chance she'd dreamed about, waited for. She would be Holden Fortune's girl. He'd drive her to school, walk her to classes, sit with her at lunch, take her to dances...maybe even give her his class ring, something he hadn't done with any of his other girlfriends.

She would never treat him the way they had. Never.

"Holden," she said.

He lifted his head, bleary-eyed and unfocused.

"I could be that kind of girl...for you."

His smile was slow and slightly crooked. "No, you couldn't..."

She leaned up and pressed her lips to his again. This time when he put his tongue in her mouth, she touched it with hers. And when his hand slipped under her sweater she pressed herself against its touch.

Lifting his head away, his voice gruff, he whispered, "Let's...let's go up to my room." He held out a hand.

She got up, helped him to his feet, and then, with effort, up the stairs.

He started kissing her again before they even stumbled through his bedroom door. She fell backward, Holden still wrapped around her, and landed on the bed. It was fast, brief, messy, and not at all what she had expected. All so clinical. He didn't hug her or hold her, caress her or kiss her. He shoved her panties down, and pushed up her skirt. Didn't even take off his jeans. Just lowered them and—did it. It hurt at first, and then the pain eased, and it was all over.

But…it couldn't be. Surely there was more to sex than…than *that*.

Holden lay on top of her, very still, breathing deeply and steadily. Lucinda shook him. "Holden?" He didn't respond and tears welled up in her eyes. "Holden, please…"

He grumbled and rolled off her. A glance at his face made her realize that he was out cold, and no amount of shaking or pleading would wake him up. She dragged the stained sheet out from under him, wrapped herself in it, snatched up her clothes and ran into the bathroom attached to his bedroom, slamming the door behind her. It had been awful. Embarrassing, humiliating, and awful.

She cried for a few minutes. Then told herself to stop it. She'd wanted this. And…and it was worth it. Maybe. After all, being Holden Fortune's girlfriend was all she'd dreamed about for a long time now. Well, almost all. She dreamed about being a doctor, too, ever since her mom died five years ago. Now, one of those dreams…had come true. Taking a breath, sighing deeply, she dried her tears, and turned on the water. By the time she got herself cleaned up and dressed, she was feeling a little bit better about what had happened between her and Holden tonight. There had been no tenderness...but that was only because he'd been drinking. Tomorrow, everything would be different. Tomorrow...

She crept back into the bedroom and bent over him to plant a gentle kiss on his cheek. "I love you, Holden Fortune," she whispered. "I'll love you forever." Then she hurried through the huge house, back to the front door, all without meeting anyone, and drove home floating on a cloud. So what if it was a rather dark, ominous-looking cloud? It would look brighter tomorrow.

Holden didn't call in the morning to offer her a ride to school. She'd expected him to, but she battled the disappointment by telling herself he might be sick from all that liquor and was maybe just sleeping it off.

But when she got off the bus at school, she looked up to see Holden's shiny red Corvette pulling in. Both doors opened at once. Holden hopped out of one door, smiling. Tiffany Lambert came out the other door. They met in the front, and Holden put his arm around her.

Lucinda just stood there on the sidewalk, staring until there was too much moisture in her eyes to see through as the two of them walked toward her, arm in arm. She couldn't move. The pain in her chest was too big, choking her. She could barely even breathe.

"Hey, Lucy," Holden said.

Lucinda blinked the stinging tears from her eyes.

She wanted to run. But instead she just stood there and said, "Hi."

"Thanks for the ride home last night. You really pulled my fat out of the fire."

"No problem," she managed to choke out.

"I hope I wasn't an idiot."

She only frowned at him, not sure what to say, how to act.

"I mean, I was pretty wasted. I don't remember a damn thing after getting into the car."

She blinked, and rasped, "You...you don't?"

"Total blackout," he said. "Anyway, thanks. If you ever need a favor, you know who to ask, okay?"

She lowered her head as fresh tears came flooding from nowhere. "Yeah. Sure."

"Come on, Holden. You promised me a doughnut in the cafeteria before homeroom," Tiffany teased in that voice of hers that could make even the most mundane statement sound like a come-on. And then the two walked away.

Just walked away.

Lucinda ran for the nearest girls' room, where she threw up. Then she just sank down onto the floor, pulled her knees to her chest, and cried.

She was still there when the school nurse came looking an hour later. She spent the rest of that day at home in bed, wondering if she would ever recover from the mess Holden Fortune had made of her heart.

It was several weeks later when she realized the damage Holden had done had not been to her heart alone. When she collapsed in agonizing pain and was rushed to the hospital, bleeding uncontrollably. When she awoke from emergency surgery, sore and groggy and confused. When the doctor told her the pregnancy had been ectopic—that the fetus had been growing in her fallopian tube, and the tube had ruptured. That one of her ovaries had had to be removed to save her life. That her chances of conceiving a child in the future were cut in half.

She lay there in the hospital bed, in pain, afraid, and for the most part, alone. Oh, her father was there, but he'd been distant since her mother had died. He asked no questions, demanded no explanations. Just stayed by her side, looking heartbroken.

And all the while, Lucinda thought, Holden was out there somewhere, driving around in his expensive car with his pretty girlfriend, spending his father's money as if there were no tomorrow. That night with him had changed her life forever. But he was so wrapped up in himself that he didn't even know it. He didn't even remember....

She would hate Holden Fortune for as long as she lived.

One

Everyone was here for the party. Holden, looking angry about something—and without a woman on his arm for once. He *must really* be out of sorts. Matthew and Claudia, beaming with pride over *their* child. And why not? Bryan Fortune was lucky, born into billions, with half the county here to celebrate his christening. Even that snooty OB-GYN who'd delivered him was here. Lucinda whatever her name was.

Maria Cassidy used the back door. "The servants' entrance," though the phony Fortune family would never be heard referring to it that way. It was how they thought of it, though. Oh, they put on a good show. But that's all it was. A show. The way the Fortune men had used Maria's mother, Lily, and then tossed her aside was proof of that. The way Ryan Fortune was still using her. But Ryan's guise as the kindly patriarch didn't fool Maria. Nor did his claim to be madly in love with her mother. If he'd loved her, he would never have dumped her thirty years ago, leaving her alone and pregnant.

He'd fathered Maria's brother, Cole. Him, or that philandering brother of his, Cameron. Maria couldn't be certain. Her mother refused to say exactly what had happened when she'd worked in the Fortunes' household as a girl. She hadn't told anyone, not even Ryan, whom she'd "found again" after thirty years. None of the Fortunes knew about the crown-shaped birthmark Maria's brother bore, identifying him clearly as one of their own. And Cole said he didn't care.

But Maria cared. Part of the Fortunes' wealth rightfully belonged to her family. To her mother for years of suffering and silence. To her brother who'd been denied his share. Cameron and Ryan Fortune were to blame, she was certain, for her family being cut out. But Cameron was already dead, and burning in hell if there was any justice in the world. And Ryan...he would soon be in a hell of his own, a hell of Maria's creation. And his whole rich family would be there with him.

Maria clutched the tiny bundle in her arms closer, jiggling him gently as she slipped past the kitchen unnoticed. Little James was blessedly quiet. Good. She didn't want to spoil her surprise by giving it away too soon. In the kitchen, that witch housekeeper, Rosita Perez, made enough noise to cover any James might make anyway. Barking orders to the staff as if she were one of the Fortunes. She'd never liked Maria. Always acted superior, even though she was just a glorified maid. Chief cook and bottle washer to the great Fortune clan. Had been forever, even thirty years ago when Maria's mother had worked in this very house, in that very kitchen. And one year ago, when Maria had done the same.

Just like her mother, Maria had managed to sleep with a couple of Fortune males. Unlike her mother, she'd had a motive…to bear a Fortune child of her own and claim what her entire family should have claimed long ago. A fair share. And though Maria's attempts had been unsuccessful at first, she'd found a way. Unorthodox, perhaps, but a way all the same. Just like her mother, Maria Cassidy had given birth to a Fortune child. Little James bore the distinctive, hereditary crown-shaped birthmark on the small of his back. Just like Maria's brother, Cole.

That part of her plan was complete. This was the next step. Maria intended to tell the whole world who had fathered her child, and claim what was rightfully hers. A piece of the Fortune pie. A big piece.

She slipped through the old pantry to the back stairs and went up them, knowing every inch of this estate by heart. The nursery was at the end of the hall, and that was where Maria headed, on tiptoe, careful not to be seen.

When she stepped into the lavish nursery, she grimaced. ¡Dios! That Ryan's grandchild Bryan should have all this while her own son had nothing! While her own brother had worked his tail off for everything he'd ever achieved. While her own mother had gone without all these years.…

The crib at the farthest end of the nursery was hand-tooled light oak, and probably worth a bundle. The walls had been elaborately decorated with bright colors, and building blocks and teddy bears. The rocking chair was an antique. And the bassinet… God, the bassinet…

Maria went to it and ran her hands over the gleaming wood. It wasn't a piece of furniture. It was a work of art. "This is where you belong, James," she whispered to her son as she laid him gently inside it. "That's right, darling. Sleep. Just sleep. Mamma will be back for you when the moment is right." Bending closer, she kissed her son's silken cheek, then straightened, and stepped back into the hall, closing the door softly behind her.

She paused there, took a breath, and wondered briefly if she were making a mistake. But no. This was right. She had to do something. She couldn't let her mother go on sleeping with Ryan Fortune, believing that he loved her, believing that he would divorce that barracuda wife of his and marry Lily. He wouldn't. He'd leave her high and dry...just like before. He still hadn't acknowledged Cole as a Fortune. If he loved Lily, he would at least have owned up to having fathered her firstborn. Because even though Lily had never told him, he must at least suspect the truth. The man could add, couldn't he? Lily had given birth to Cole only eight months after running away from the Double Crown Ranch—only seven months after marrying Maria's father, big, gentle Chester Cassidy.

Well, Ryan Fortune would acknowledge James as his grandson. Maria would force him to.

It was the perfect setting for her revelation. A lavish, no-holds-barred christening party for Matthew's child, Ryan's grandchild, Bryan Fortune. But this whole clan would soon find out that they had another child to celebrate. Maria's child. James.

And he was here to take his rightful place in the world. Her son was a Fortune. And he would not be denied!

Holden Fortune was not amused. His uncle Ryan had paraded no less than a dozen "nice young ladies" past him tonight in a thinly veiled effort at match-making that was doomed to failure. He'd just intro-duced yet another; a petite little thing that reminded Holden of a mouse. Holden's brisk greeting had sent her skittering off in search of someone friendlier. Un-cle Ryan was scowling at him in a fairly good imper-sonation of Heston's scowling at Brynner in *The Ten Commandments*.

"I don't understand you, Holden. We all know you like women—"

"Ever the king of understatement," Holden re-marked dryly, taking another sip of bourbon and branch.

"So, what's the problem? Every girl I've brought over here has been attractive, and nice and—"

"I don't want attractive and nice, Uncle Ryan. I want drop-dead gorgeous and very, *very* naughty. Es-pecially tonight. 'Nice' just isn't gonna cut it tonight."

Around him were more people than he'd seen at the last cattlemen's convention. Two-thirds of them fam-ily. All the colorful Mexican rugs had been rolled back and the double patio doors thrown wide. The crowd spilled out into the courtyard where Rosita had piled food on tables and Matthew manned the barbecue pit. The smells were damned mouthwatering. Yet Holden had no appetite.

"You're going to have to stop this," Ryan ordered in his head-honcho tone.

"Stop what?"

"You know damned well what. Holden you are *not* your father. You don't need to go through life trying to live up to his reputation as a playboy. You can settle down, find a good woman, make a life—''

"Yeah, dear ol' Daddy made sure I would, didn't he? Went so far as to write it into an ironclad will that I can't inherit my fair share until I do.''

Ryan nodded solemnly. "And just why do you think my brother did that, Holden?''

Holden shrugged. "Because he was a bastard?''

Ryan lowered his head quickly, probably to hide a hint of amusement. "I like to think my brother realized the error of his ways, in the end. I like to think he wrote those conditions into his will so his firstborn son wouldn't make the same mistakes he did.''

Holden sighed deeply and shook his head. "Therein lies the problem, Uncle Ryan. If I marry some decent woman, I will be doing just that. Repeating my father's mistakes. Ruining a good woman's life by tying her to me. For God's sake, look at my mother.''

Ryan did. He glanced up, scanned the crowd. Holden followed his gaze and found Mary Ellen Fortune standing alone, a drink in her hand, staring up at the portrait of her dead husband. Fifty-six, and still a knockout. She'd kept her figure. Her red hair didn't have a streak of gray in it, and since Cameron's death, she'd even had it cut into a more modern style that bobbed just above her shoulders and moved when she did.

"She was wasted on him,'' Holden said. "He made her miserable. And I wouldn't want to follow in his footsteps by making some other good woman equally unhappy. Unfortunately, unless I do, I don't inherit a dime.''

Ryan looked back at Holden again. "Your lawyers…"

"I spoke to them an hour ago. It's over. The judge upheld the will as is. No more appeals, no more contesting it. It's over."

Ryan sighed deeply. "I'm sorry, Holden."

"Yeah. So am I." Holden took a long pull from his glass.

"But just because your father was a womanizing louse, doesn't mean you have to be."

"Too late, Uncle Ryan. I already am." He glanced up at his father's portrait. The golden boy looked down at him. His smile seemed to Holden almost mocking. Blond hair, blue eyes, clean-cut, all-American, rich SOB. It was like looking into a mirror. Holden lifted his glass in mock salute. "You win, Dad." Then he downed the contents. As he did, he spotted exactly what he'd been looking for. Someone he could take home, take to bed, and ravage in every possible way until he got this will stuff out of his system.

She was standing near the barbecue pit, talking to Matthew and his wife Claudia. Her back was to Holden, but he could see enough. She was…exquisite. Jet hair, so black it seemed almost blue in the slanting afternoon sun. So smooth…like satin. He'd bet her eyes were dark, too. Ebon, and slanted. Native American eyes, to go with that bronze skin. Slender, yeah, with just the right curves to her. She was hot. Dressed to hide it, sure. Forest-green silk suit. But that skirt was short, and tight, and her legs looked as if they never ended. She'd be a wild woman in bed.

"Now there's someone I'd like to meet," he muttered to Ryan, and when his uncle didn't answer, Holden turned to see he'd lost Ryan's attention. It had been stolen the second Lily Cassidy had entered the room. As usual, Uncle Ryan only had eyes for the dark beauty who'd captured his heart thirty years ago, and only recently come back into his life. Lily's heart was in her eyes as she crossed the room and Ryan took her hands. If anyone in the world deserved to be happy, it was those two. Holden wished for the millionth time that Sophia would just agree to the divorce and set his uncle free. Everyone knew it was the money she'd been after all along.

With a sigh, he returned his attention to the other dark beauty, the one out in the courtyard with his cousin the doctor. He supposed he ought to be grateful for at least one of his father's traits—he'd never yet met a woman who would tell him no. And from the looks of her, he didn't expect this one to be the first. Holden exchanged his empty glass for a full one at the portable bar set up in the great room, and sauntered out through the wide-open patio doors to the pit where Matthew tended the ribs. He pretended great interest in the cooking process, all the while keeping one eye on the lucky woman he'd chosen to ease his misery tonight. "Anything I can do, cousin?"

"Hand me that platter. This batch is done."

Holden snagged the platter and held it obediently as Matthew began piling ribs on it. The smell was heavenly. But Holden was more interested in watching the two women—Claudia, Matthew's wife, and that hot little number she was talking to. She'd turned a little as he'd come out. He still couldn't get a good look at her face. The platter grew heavier in his hand. "So,

Claudia, where's the guest of honor? Not sleeping through his own party, is he?''

Claudia glanced his way with a smile. She and Matthew had never seemed happier. His cousin had something—something Holden would never have. A wife who adored him. A family. A future. Holden felt a flash of envy and a hint of self-pity. He squelched both.

"That's exactly what he's doing," Claudia said. "All the excitement of the christening wore him right out."

The darker one looked his way. He caught her eye, but she quickly averted her face. There was something familiar about her. "You...haven't introduced me to your friend."

Matthew suppressed a chuckle. Claudia just shook her head. "Oh, come on, Holden. You know Lucinda." At Holden's blank look she went on. "Lucinda Brightwater? From high school?"

And then, even as he blinked in shock, the woman spoke.

"I'm afraid I never made that much of an impression on your cousin, Claudia," she said, her voice slightly chilly. Yet deep and rich, like warmed honey. At last, she faced him.

Holden caught his breath. But this knockout couldn't possibly be that untouchable, pristine, painfully shy girl he remembered. "Lucy Brightwater?" he asked, failing to hide his surprise.

She lifted her dark brows. "The one and only." She started to turn away. "I think I see someone I know. If you'll excuse me."

"Hold on a minute!" Holden automatically moved

closer, gripping her arm lightly. "Hey, it's been years. Give a guy a break, huh?"

She looked at him, her gaze icy, before it dipped to his hand on her arm. Her message was clear.

He let go immediately. And the beautiful woman walked away. Lowering his chin, Holden sighed. "She sure grew up touchy. Gorgeous, though."

"She's not your type," Claudia said. "As I recall, you made that fact painfully obvious to her back in school."

He knew she was right, but he'd be damned if he'd admit it. "Shoot, if she'd looked like that back in school—"

"I think that's the point, cousin," Matthew volunteered. "You're tipping the platter."

Holden straightened the platter and a rib fell off. Shaking her head, Claudia came forward and took the dish from him. Holden eyed her. "Besides, I don't remember being nasty to her in high school. At least, not enough to merit that icy reception." Anyway, he'd had his reasons for steering clear of Lucy back then. Reasons...that all still existed. So why didn't he just drop it? Why was he still watching her weave her way through the crowded great room? Why was he still running off at the mouth? "I always admired her. She...reminded me of Mom in some odd way."

"She had a huge crush on you back then, Holden."

"That's right... That's right. I used to see her hanging around at practice sometimes, watching me." He remembered more than that, too. He remembered that he'd decided she was far too good for the likes of him. She probably still was.

"I suppose thoroughly ignoring a girl who's not up

to your standards is something you do so often you're barely conscious of it anymore,'' Claudia said.

Ignoring her, Holden stared across the crowded room to where Lucy Brightwater was now chatting with Ryan and Lily. She looked a bit like Lily. Same dark coloring, same dramatic black eyes. Damn, no wonder Ryan had been in love with Lily for thirty-some-odd years. A woman like that...

"I'm sure as hell not ignoring her now,'' he heard himself mutter.

"Well, you sure as hell ought to be,'' Claudia snapped. "Leave her alone, Holden. She's not a one-night-stand kind of woman.''

"No. No, I remember that about her. She was always pretty...'' He shook his head. "Man, she sure grew into her looks.''

"There's a lot more to Lucinda Brightwater than the way she looks. As there is with most women, not that you've ever bothered to look any deeper than the surface.''

Holden shrugged. "Fine. You want to start listing her stellar qualities, go ahead. I'm listening.'' And interested, he thought. In fact, he was dying to know what Lucinda in the Sky Brightwater had been up to all these years.

Claudia narrowed her eyes at him, then shrugged. "Fine, I will. Lucinda is kind, compassionate and caring. She's intelligent and accomplished and sensitive, and a casual fling with a man like you could do a lot of damage to a woman like her. Leave her alone, Holden.''

As she turned and strode away to set the heaping platter on a table, Holden sent a confused glance at his cousin. "You'd think I was the devil himself, the way she acts."

"Some might say you are," Matthew said. "Claudia's a little protective of Lucinda. They got pretty close during the pregnancy and all."

Holden tilted his head, lifted a brow.

"Lucinda is Claudia's doctor. Works over at Red Rock General."

Holden blinked. "She's a *doctor?*" He looked her way once more. Damn, she didn't look like any doctor he'd ever seen. "Maybe it's time I make an appointment. I must be overdue for a physical…or something." He was only half kidding.

"Hey, I'm offended! I thought I was your favorite doctor. Besides, you'd never get in to see Lucinda…you don't have the right equipment." Matthew grinned at Holden's puzzled expression. "She's an OB-GYN." Matthew said. "She delivered Bryan. And she and Claudia sort of…bonded."

"That's the Dr. Brightwater Claudia was always talking about," Holden said as a lightbulb finally flashed on in his mind. He hadn't made the connection until now.

"The one and only," Matthew said, echoing Lucinda's earlier words. "And she's not the kind of woman who would enjoy being judged on the basis of her looks."

"Then she shouldn't go around looking like that," Holden said.

"Give it up, cousin. You don't stand a chance with her. Go find some bimbo to charm into your love nest. That woman is out of your league."

Holden finished his drink in a gulp and set down

the empty glass. "Yeah. That's pretty much what I always thought, too. But that doesn't mean I can't talk to her, does it?"

Mistake, his mind cautioned him. *Big, big mistake.*

"I'm sorry, Claudia." Lucinda Brightwater was still a bit shaky. She hadn't wanted to come to this party. No, that wasn't true. She *had* wanted to come. For Claudia and Matthew. For little Bryan. What she *hadn't* wanted was to run into Holden Fortune. The man who had taken her virginity one drunken night so long ago she should have been over it long before now. A night that had meant everything to her. A night with repercussions that were still resonating through her life.

A night that had obviously meant less than nothing to him.

She was not an awkward teenager anymore. She was not the too smart, too tall, too skinny girl who didn't quite fit in. And she certainly wasn't the same girl who'd been heart-and-soul in love with the most popular boy in school. A boy who hadn't so much as returned her shy hello when they'd passed in the halls. She was a doctor now. She'd grown into her body and become comfortable, even confident, with her looks.

So how could a brief encounter with Holden Fortune reduce her once again to a quivering mass of nerve endings, all of which seemed to be standing on end? She'd told herself that if she ran into him she would feel nothing but coldness—and a bit of her long-time resentment for the mess he'd made of her life so long ago.

Instead, she felt so many emotions she couldn't

name them all. Anger, shame…and still a hint of that old attraction to a man who was never anything but bad for her. Poison.

"You have nothing to apologize for," Claudia said softly. "My husband's cousin puts on a good show, Lucinda, but he's truly not as bad as he seems."

"You're forgetting," Lucinda said with a slightly wry look, "I knew him in high school."

Claudia tilted her head. "Did…something *happen* between you and Holden back then?"

"What a crazy question!" Lucinda averted her gaze. "Why on earth would you ask me something like that?"

"Well, you seem awfully…angry with him over something. And it has been a long time…."

Lucinda nodded. "You're right, it has, and my mood really doesn't have a thing to do with Holden." It was a lie, but not entirely. She'd been feeling like hell for weeks now. She'd get the results of her ultrasound test tomorrow, and she was dreading what she'd hear. She had a pretty fair idea about what was going on with her body.

"I probably shouldn't have taken it out on him," she said, but she didn't mean it.

"What *is* bothering you, Lucinda?"

She shook her head. "Oh, the usual. You know, with every baby I deliver it seems I hear my biological clock ticking louder than before."

Claudia smiled. "Got that urge, huh?"

"I've had that urge for some time now. And my time's running out."

"Don't be silly. You're only…"

"Thirty-four," she said, lowering her eyes to hide

the fear she knew she couldn't hide. "And then there's the clinic."

"Still can't get the funding, huh?"

Lucinda shook her head. "Health care for lower income women around here is practically nonexistent. And my big plans to change that state of things don't seem to be going anywhere."

"I don't see why you won't just let Matthew and I back you."

"I need several backers, not just one. The amount I need to get this clinic up and running is too much to expect one person to give. And taking money from friends—especially the kind of money we're talking about here—is never a good idea, Claudia. You know how I feel about that. Besides, the Fortunes aren't the only wealthy family in Texas. I want to do this on my own. I just have to convince the local bigshots to open up their pockets for a good cause."

"Just know you can count on us if you need to," Claudia said.

Lucinda nodded and squeezed her friend's hand. "I do know. And I'm grateful."

"Come on," Claudia said, tugging Lucinda toward the back of the room and the wide, curving staircase. "Let's go up and see if Bryan's ready to make his big entrance."

"Hey, hold on a minute. We'll come with you," a voice called from behind.

Lucinda stiffened, because it was Holden's voice. The voice that could still send delicious shivers up her spine yet make her want to claw his eyes out all at the same time. She turned, fixing a false smile onto her face as Holden and Matthew joined them at the foot of the stairs.

Maria had been quietly observing all of them, watching the women parade around in their expensive clothes, perfect hair, glamorous nails and real jewels. Watching the men, who watched the women. Rich bastards, all of them. When it looked as if the party was in full swing, and most of the guests had arrived, Maria slipped away again, up to the nursery to collect James. It was time for the big announcement. Time to watch them all pale with shock when they realized that she had mothered one of their own. That she wouldn't be content to be merely tolerated or seen as a former servant, or as the daughter of Ryan Fortune's whore. No. She'd be one of them now.

She slipped into the nursery, and leaned over the bassinet, cooing softly. Then she went still, because all that lay inside was the rumpled, down-soft blanket, and a large sheet of paper.

"James?" she whispered. What…

A soft gurgling noise made her turn her head sharply toward the massive crib at the far end of the room. That was it. Someone must have moved the baby. She quickly went to the crib, only to stop dead again. It wasn't James staring up at her with wide, baby-blue eyes and a toothless, dribbly smile. It was Bryan. Matthew's *legitimate* son.

Oh, God, where was James?

Her heart in her throat, Maria rushed back to the bassinet. Only then did she begin to panic. That sheet of paper seemed to stare up at her, daring her to look at it, to read what it said.

With the tip of a fingernail, she lifted the top fold.

We have taken Bryan Fortune. He will be returned unharmed, as soon as you have delivered fifty million dollars in cash.

"Fifty million..." Maria whispered. Kidnapped! Her son—her James—had been kidnapped! Mistaken for Bryan Fortune. Whoever had done this probably hadn't even noticed the other baby in the crib across the room. Maria hadn't when she'd first come in.

Fifty million dollars. Who would give fifty million dollars for an illegitimate little boy like James? Not the Fortune family. Even if they knew he was one of their own, even if Maria could somehow prove it to them...no, because James's appearance in this family would throw their golden lives into chaos. They'd never pay. They'd let the kidnappers sell him or...or worse.

Maria's throat went dry as she backed away from the bassinet and the cruel reality that was forcing its way into her mind. There was no way to get her baby back. No way...

Her back touched the crib, and the other child inside it cooed and chirped at her. She turned.

What if the Fortunes believed that it was Bryan who'd been taken? No one knew James even existed. What if...

What if she took little Bryan...for just a little while? Just until the ransom was paid and James was safe again. Then she'd switch the babies back, make it all right. Somehow....

Somehow.

She bent over the crib, gathering Bryan Fortune into her arms. "You won't mind so much, will you, little one? I'll take good care of you, and you'll be back with your mamma in no time at all. It's not so much to ask, is it? To save my baby's life?"

The baby smiled as if in response, and Maria wrapped him in a blanket and snuggled him close, smelling his baby smell as tears welled up in her eyes. "God, this all went so wrong…so wrong…"

She paused on the way out, licking her lips as she looked once more at the note in the bassinet. This had to look real, it had to be convincing. Cradling the baby close with one arm, she quickly picked up the note, using the edge of a receiving blanket to cover her fingers. No fingerprints. She mustn't leave a trace. She carried the note to Bryan's crib, dropped it inside, and hurried away before she could change her mind.

Two

As they walked up the stairs, Claudia and Matthew fell into step, side by side, hand in hand, leading the way. Leaving Lucinda to walk at Holden's side. And the whole time, she swore he never took his eyes off her. She got the feeling he had some special X-ray vision that could see right through her clothes. Then again, that view was one he'd seen before—and it hadn't made much of an impression on him then.

He certainly did seem to be paying attention now, though.

Men. She wished she could think like they did, feel like they did. All she wanted was a relationship that could develop into something...something like Claudia had with Matthew. She wanted a husband, a baby...

God, she wanted a baby so much....

But all her efforts at relationships had turned out in one of two ways. Either the man she was seeing wanted no commitment at all or he wanted too much of one. Mostly the latter. One man after another had bid her adios when it became apparent that she wasn't willing to give up her practice, or her plans of building a clinic, to devote her full attention to him.

Maybe she didn't need a man at all. Maybe all she needed was a willing sperm donor. A one-night stand.

"So, Lucy," Holden said. "What are you doing after the party?"

She blinked at his interruption of her rather uncharacteristic and slightly shocking train of thought. She told herself not to imagine his gold-blond hair and sky-blue eyes on a little baby. The baby that she'd lost all those years ago—maybe the only baby she would ever have a part in creating. But she imagined it anyway, and an evil thought entered her mind. About poetic justice. About his potential as a sperm donor. It was totally unlike her to think of such things as trickery and deception. But where Holden Fortune was concerned, it did seem justified.

And she already knew he was fond of one-night stands. "Um, why do you ask?"

They'd reached the top of the stairs. Claudia and Matthew were already heading down the hall, but Holden stopped there, turning to face her. "I don't know, really. I guess...I'd like to make up for being such a jerk to you in high school."

She felt the blush creeping into her face. "So you *do* remember."

"No, I really don't. I mean, I remember you, but not the part about being a jerk. But Claudia says..." He stopped. "I said the wrong thing."

Lucinda shook her head. For a moment she'd thought maybe that special, horrible, wonderful night hadn't been erased from his mind almost before it had ended. But she'd been wrong. It had.

"Look, I drank a lot in high school," he blurted, trying to explain his way out of an awkward moment. "Dated a lot, too."

"I wouldn't call it *dating*." He gave her a sheepish smile.

"You haven't changed a bit, have you, Holden?"

"Sure I have. And to tell you the truth, I'm dying to know what I did to make you seem so...unfriendly now. Why don't you have dinner with me tonight and we can...talk."

She narrowed her eyes and stared at him. Why not? If he wanted to wine her and dine her and take her to bed, why not go along with it? Maybe she'd get what she wanted out of the deal. A baby. Of her own, with no man and no strings attached. Lord knew, Holden wouldn't be the type to demand joint custody. He couldn't even commit to a steady girlfriend, much less a child. Hell, he might not even remember having fathered her baby after the fact.

"I just might take you up on that."

He frowned at her, wondering at her tone, she was sure. She'd made the words sound as if they were more threat than promise. "Lucy, what in hell did I do to make you so mad at me after all this time?"

Before she could even begin to formulate an answer, a heart-wrenching scream echoed through the house. Lucinda turned her head sharply. "That came from the nursery!" she said, and a second later she and Holden were running full-tilt.

Holden forgot everything else when he lunged through the nursery door and saw Claudia sitting on the floor sobbing, a sheet of paper clutched in one trembling fist, while the other was pressed to her heart. The sight of her almost floored him. White. Deathly, sickly white. She looked as if something had just

sucked every ounce of life from her body. Even her
pale blond hair, usually wavy and full, seemed to hang
limply around her petite face.

"No!" A fist smashed through the nursery wall,
leaving a big hole in the plaster. Matthew swore and
jerked his hand free, knuckles dusted white, skinned
up and bleeding. "This isn't happening!"

"My baby...oh, God, my baby," Claudia wailed.

"The baby," Lucinda whispered, rushing first to the
bassinet just inside the door, and then across the room
toward the crib, thoughts of SIDS—sudden infant
death syndrome—foremost in her mind. "Is something
wrong with the—" She froze at the crib. Then slowly
turned wide eyes on Holden. "Where is Bryan?"

Claudia bowed double, her head in her lap, her
shoulders shaking with violent sobs. Matthew strode
toward the door. "Lock this place up, Holden," he
said, his voice coarse as cherry bark. "Nobody leaves.
You hear me? Nobody leaves!"

"Dammit, Matthew, what's going on here? Where
the hell are you going?" Holden demanded, stepping
into his cousin's path.

But Matthew shoved past him, knocking Holden
aside so hard his shoulder slammed into the wall. "To
get the keys to Dad's gun cabinet," Matthew rasped,
and hit the hall running.

Holden turned to give chase, then glanced back at
Claudia on the floor, not sure who needed his help
more right now.

Lucy knelt beside Claudia, nodded at him once to
go ahead, then said, "Holden, wait."

He turned to see that she'd pried that sheet of paper

out of Claudia's hand and was staring at it. "Oh, my God," she whispered.

"What is it, Lucy?"

Lucinda lifted her stunned gaze to meet Holden's. "It…it's a ransom note. My God, Holden, the baby's been kidnapped!"

He felt the shock as if someone had kicked him in the teeth. Then he shook it off. "I've gotta get hold of my cousin before he kills somebody."

"Go on. I'll take care of Claudia." And she was. Even as Holden hesitated, half afraid to leave the petite blonde who looked as if she was on the verge of a breakdown, Lucinda spoke to her, got her to her feet. Anchoring Claudia to her side with a strength that surprised him, she looked up and nodded at Holden once more. "Go on."

He went.

He hit the bottom of the stairs about the time he heard glass being smashed. He didn't have to look to know the sound was coming from Ryan's den, or the gun cabinet that took up most of one wall in that room. People were starting to look alarmed, furrowed brows turning his way. Holden banged into his brother on the way to the den.

"What the hell—"

"Logan. Listen, seal this place off. Don't let anyone leave, you understand?"

"But—"

"Someone's taken Bryan. Block every exit—"

"Bryan?" Logan looked stricken, his bronzed skin paling. One hand pushed through his sun-streaked brown hair.

Holden waved a hand in the air, signaling Matthew's brothers, Zane and Dallas. As they surged toward him with worried frowns, Holden saw Rosita talking to her husband, Ruben, who was one of their most trusted ranch hands and almost as much a part of the family as Rosita was. Holden waved him over, as well. "Have the guys help you, Logan. I have to stop Matthew before he—"

A woman squealed and Holden turned to see Matthew come bursting into the great room with Ryan's twelve-gauge Remington in his hands. Matthew's eyes were wild, and he was waving that shotgun around in a way that made Holden hope to God it wasn't loaded.

"Where is he!" Matthew demanded. "Give him to me now!"

"Matthew!" Holden surged forward, gripping his cousin's shoulders, just as Uncle Ryan came from another direction to grab his shotgun away from his son. For a man his age, he was still in peak condition, and he didn't have much trouble.

"What in the world has gotten into you, Matthew?" Ryan asked.

Matthew stared into his father's eyes for a moment and then his face just collapsed. His body seemed damn close to following suit. He sank against Ryan, who suddenly wore a look of extreme fear as he put his arms around his son and held him hard. Ryan's eyes met Holden's over Matthew's shuddering shoulders, a question in them.

"The baby's been kidnapped," Holden explained, only to see Ryan's eyes fill with even more horror.

"God, no!" Then, shaking his head, he slapped his son's back. "We'll pay whatever they ask, son. Give them the whole damned spread and the company along with it. Everything, you hear me, boy? We'll get Bryan back. I promise you. Whatever they want, they'll have. Whatever it takes to get my grandson back here safe and sound.''

Ryan Fortune lowered his head. "And then...then, they'll suffer like they've never suffered before. Whoever did this is going to pay, believe me.''

Lily gasped, hurrying forward, clutching Mary Ellen's arm and pulling her along to Ryan's side. Holden was certain both women had overheard what he'd said—apparently, at least enough to realize what had happened. A second later Holden's mother broke away from Lily's grip to head back into the crowded great room, but Lily kept coming.

Holden stepped away from Matthew when Lucy appeared at the bottom of the stairs and strode purposefully to his side. She didn't hesitate, just stuck Matthew's arm with a hypodermic, and even as Matthew jerked his head around to object, it was obvious to Holden he was starting to feel the effect.

Above it all, Holden heard his mother, taking charge. Ordering everyone to remain calm, to sit down, to keep order.

"I assure you all," Mary Ellen said in her Lauren Bacall voice, "everything is under control. We'll explain all of this in just a few moments, but for now, I'm afraid I have to ask that no one leave. A crime has been committed. I've just spoken with Sheriff Grayhawk. He's on his way here now, and asks that everyone stay just until he gets here and has a chance to speak with each of you.''

The crowd quieted. People muttered, asked questions, but the panic seemed to ease. No one could see through Mary Ellen Fortune's facade if she didn't want them to. No one but Holden. He knew his mother better than anyone. She had to be falling apart inside. And yet she'd already contacted the sheriff and was in complete control. Emotions well hidden. Ever the perfect hostess. Living with his bastard of a father had certainly trained her well, hadn't it?

He glanced at Lucy Brightwater, and felt a surge of misgiving. He shouldn't have asked her out. She may look as if she'd changed, but a lady was a lady. And just because she no longer looked like the sensitive, vulnerable, fragile thing she'd been, didn't mean she wasn't.

"Your mother has everything under control here," Lucinda said. "Help me get your cousin upstairs."

"What about Claudia?" Holden hefted a wilting Matthew into his arms as he asked the question.

"I sedated her, too. She's sleeping now. God, Holden, who could've done this?"

"I don't know." Holden looked behind him as he mounted the stairs, staring at the stunned, restless crowd. At his brother and cousins, guarding the doors like bulldogs. At Rosita, one hand on her heart and tears streaming from dark Mexican eyes down over her plump cheeks. She dabbed at them with her apron, while her husband stood near another door, watching her worriedly. Ryan clung to Lily and Lily to Ryan. And Mary Ellen held them all together. She was the rock of this family and always had been.

"You didn't leave Claudia alone, did you?" Holden asked suddenly.

"Of course not," Lucinda said. "Vanessa is with her."

"Good." He carried his cousin up the stairs. Matthew was still muttering, but semi-conscious now. Lucinda led the way, opened the bedroom door, and preceded Holden into it.

"Holden!" Vanessa was on her feet and flinging her arms around Holden's neck almost before he could finish lowering Matthew to the bed.

Holden hugged his cousin, and then stepped back to brush away her tears and smooth her hair. "It's gonna be okay, Vanessa."

"When I find out who took my nephew, he's going to be one hurting son of a—"

"That kind of talk isn't going to help anyone right now," Holden told her gently.

Vanessa sighed, and pushed a hand through her short, sassy hair. "Maybe not. But I mean it." She leaned over the bed, smoothing her big brother's hair. "Is Matthew okay?"

"He's just sleeping," Lucinda explained. "I had to sedate him."

"I don't know what I'd have done if you hadn't been here, Lucinda. God, Claudia was so—"

"I'm just glad you happened to walk by the bedroom when you did. I couldn't have handled her alone."

Frowning, Holden looked at Lucy, then looked again. Her dark hair was tousled, and there was a scratch beading with red droplets across one cheek. He quickly rounded the bed that stood between them. He hadn't got a glimpse of the scratch until now. He'd been behind her up the stairs, and before that his cousin's dead weight in his arms had blocked his view. Only as he neared her now did he notice how messed up she was. Then he saw the lamp that was smashed to bits on the floor behind her, and the table lying on its side.

"My God, what happened?" He palmed her cheek, tipped her face up for a closer look.

"She got a little hysterical. It's a perfectly normal reaction and I should have expected it."

"You're bleeding." Holden snagged a tissue from the decorative box on the nearby dresser, and dabbed the blood away, very gently.

Lucinda rolled her eyes in a mimicry of sarcasm. "Which of us is the doctor, again?"

He offered her a small, shaky smile, and continued dabbing. "Right now, I am. Are you hurt anywhere else?"

She lowered her eyes, shook her head.

Holden thought maybe she was lying, but he didn't press the issue. She was tougher than she looked, reminding him yet again of his mother, the way she'd jumped in and handled things without batting an eye. That calm, deliberate action. That core of strength that didn't show until a crisis hit.

He liked her, he realized slowly. But then, he always had. She looked up, meeting his eyes, briskly taking the tissue from his hand. "We'd better get back downstairs."

God, she was as shaken by Bryan's abduction as he was. It showed in her eyes.

"No. We'll stay here. Keep an eye on Matthew and Claudia."

"But the sheriff..."

"Will know where to find us when he's ready to talk to us." He turned toward Vanessa, who was eyeing him oddly. "Go on down and let the family know where we are. And maybe bring Lucy up a drink if you get a chance." His gaze went back to Lucy's face. It was pale, and she looked shaky. "Brandy. Okay?"

"Sure, Holden."

An hour later Lucinda sat in a large, cozy chair, as instructed. Holden dragged a footstool closer and, lifting her feet, propped them on it. She smiled at him for just a moment. Then closed her eyes, shook her head. "I shouldn't be sleepy at a time like this."

"It's the aftermath of chaos. You're emotionally drained. I feel the same way."

"It's like being in limbo. I keep thinking we should be doing something..."

"I know."

"And I can't remember the last time I got a full night's sleep."

"Me neither," Holden said. He glanced at the big double bed where Claudia and Matthew were out cold, side by side. "I don't imagine they'll be getting too much, either. Until Bryan's home where he belongs."

"I'll leave a prescription. They're going to need something."

"Claudia might take it. Matthew won't."

"You're probably right." Lucinda closed her eyes and let her head rest against the back of the chair.

Holden's voice came from close by, and she realized he'd pulled his harder, less comfortable chair closer to hers. "So what's been keeping you up nights, Doc?"

She didn't open her eyes. "Babies tend to come at

odd hours. And Braxton-Hicks is almost always nocturnal.''

"Braxton who?"

"False labor," she said with a slight smile.

"Ah. Right. So it's your patients keeping you awake nights, then."

"Among other things." She took a deep breath, sighed softly.

"Matthew mentioned something about a clinic you want to build." Holden stopped, waiting for her to fill him in if she wanted to.

She saw no reason not to fill the tense hours of waiting with conversation, so she told him.

"The lower income women need a clinic," she said. "Particularly the Mexican and Native American communities. There's just nothing for them. I see them all the time. They wait until they're too ill to wait any longer before they come in. Girls in their ninth month of pregnancy, coming in for their first obstetrical exam. Or worse, waiting until they're in labor." She shook her head slightly against the cushion that pillowed it. "It's got to change."

"And you're going to be the one to change it."

She nodded. "Just as soon as I can dig up a million dollars in funding, that's exactly what I'm going to do."

He was quiet for a moment. Then he said, "Why you?"

Lucinda shrugged, not even sure if his eyes were open to see it. "They're my people. I'm fortunate, so I have an obligation to give something back."

"That makes some noble kind of sense, I suppose."

"Glad you think so." She didn't like talking about

herself or her clinic to someone like him. It felt too much like hinting around for a donation, so she quickly changed the subject. "What's been keeping you awake nights, Holden Fortune? Too many visits to the salad bar at the babe buffet?"

When he didn't answer, she opened her eyes to see him staring at her, one eyebrow cocked. "'Babe buffet'?"

"Sure. I've heard you have a different course every night and still haven't managed to sample every dish in Texas."

"Sheesh. My reputation is that bad, huh?"

"Worse," she said.

"Well, it'll probably surprise you to know I'm thinking about settling down. Getting married, even."

Her eyes popped open wider and she sat up in the chair. "You've got to be kidding me."

"Nope. I'm dead serious."

Something in her belly clenched just a little. "I...didn't realize you were seeing anyone...special."

"I'm not."

"Then...then who's this woman you're planning to marry?"

Holden shrugged. "I haven't decided yet."

She frowned at him. "Excuse me?"

He sent her a look of exasperation. "My father's will came with a catch. I can't inherit until I marry a—and I quote—'woman of good reputation.'"

She tried to stifle a snort of disbelief, but it came out all the same.

"Yeah. I thought it was pretty unbelievable, too," he said.

"I am."

Holden started for the door, then paused. "Lucy...do me a favor and don't leave for a while. I'd really like to continue this conversation."

She shrugged. "If my beeper goes off, I don't have much choice in the matter," she said. "But I'll hang around as long as I can."

"Good," he said, looking at her oddly. "Good." He left the room and closed the door.

Three

"Do you mind if I give you some unsolicited advice?" Lily asked in her soft voice.

Lucinda sat back in her place, watching Claudia and Matthew closely, though she didn't expect either of them to wake anytime soon. "Advice? About what?"

"About Holden."

Lucinda blinked and quickly averted her eyes. "I don't know what you're—"

"I'm not blind, Lucinda. And you don't have what I would call a...poker face."

Lucinda shook her head slowly. "You're imagining things, Lily."

"Be careful with him," she went on. "He's trying very hard to be just like his father. And his father was...not a nice man."

Lucinda's brows went up. "You knew him well, then?"

"Cameron? I knew him. Thirty years ago when I first came here to work for the family. He and Ryan—they couldn't have been more different. Cameron used women and threw them away."

Lucinda tilted her head, facing Lily squarely. "And you think Holden is the same way?"

"I think Holden has reached a crossroads. Time will tell which path he chooses. But right now, he's dangerous, Lucinda. Particularly to a woman who might be…vulnerable to him.''

Lucinda lifted her brows. ''Well, I certainly don't fall into that category.''

With a gentle smile, Lily said, ''Good. He can't hurt you, then.''

Taking a deep breath, thinking twice before she spoke and then deciding she had no reason not to, Lucinda said, ''I thought it was Ryan you fell in love with way back then.''

''It was.''

''Then why do I get the feeling it was Cameron who broke your heart?''

Lily's eyes widened slightly before she averted them. Lucinda's beeper went off in her pocket and she grabbed for it quickly, shut it off, and looked toward the couple in the bed. But the sound hadn't pierced their drug-induced sleep. Glancing down at the beeper, she saw a familiar number on the digital readout.

''It's the hospital. I have to go. They wouldn't be calling if it wasn't an emergency.''

Lily nodded. And she looked almost…relieved. ''Go ahead. I'll be fine here.'' Lucinda glanced worriedly at Matthew and Claudia. ''If you're concerned,'' Lily went on, ''then send Ryan up on your way out.''

She nodded. ''All right. I'll do that. Tell Holden…'' She paused as Lily's brows went up. ''Never mind,'' Lucinda said, and she hurried out of the room.

It was a crazy thought. An utterly ridiculous idea. Ludicrous. But Holden couldn't get it out of his mind. It lingered there. Even while his mother was opening up the doors to admit Sam Waterman, a private security consultant Uncle Ryan had used before. Even while Sheriff Wyatt Grayhawk filled Sam in and the two of them concluded their questioning of the guests and gave the last of them the okay to leave. Even while the local cops were checking the trunks and back seats of the cars one by one before letting them pass out through the front gates.

As soon as the sheriff and Sam finished questioning him, Holden headed back upstairs to Matthew and Claudia's room. But when he burst through the door, he saw Uncle Ryan standing near the window, Lily wrapped in his arms.

They looked up when he entered, and Holden could see the tear tracks on Lily's face. Less evident, but still visible, was the worry in his uncle Ryan's. "How are they doing?" Holden asked, glancing toward the bed.

"Resting. I hate to think about what will happen when they wake." Ryan shook his head. Holden nodded in full agreement and took another look around the room.

"She had to go back to the hospital," Lily said.

He glanced at her sharply. "Who?"

Lily just scowled at him. "You know perfectly well who. Lucinda Brightwater."

"Oh. Her." Holden averted his eyes. He disliked Lily's opinion of him, though he did nothing to discourage it. She seemed to agree with his own conclusion that he was too much like his old man to be trusted. Especially with nice girls…like Lucy.

"Has the sheriff learned anything new?" Ryan asked.

"No, not yet." Holden looked at his cousin Matthew as he began to stir. "It's still so soon. Look, something's going to turn up."

Matthew's eyes opened. He looked around, disoriented, blinking. Then he closed his eyes tight again. "Oh, God, Bryan..."

"It's all right, Matthew." Lily rushed to the bedside.

"It's not all right. God, my son—" Matthew sat up in the bed, his head in his hands.

Holden went to him. Moving Lily gently aside, he took Matthew by the shoulders. "Listen up, cousin."

When Matthew didn't respond, Holden gave him a shake. Lily started to protest but Ryan held up a hand and she went still. "Dammit, Matthew, listen to me. You have to pull yourself together. Look around here. Look at your wife, for God's sake."

Matthew looked sideways at Claudia. She lay curled in the fetal position, her eyes moving rapidly beneath lightly closed lids, her hair mussed, her breathing uneven and jerky.

"She's gonna need you, Matthew. She's gonna need you solid and strong. This thing could take some time, and it's gonna be rough on her. You go falling apart, and she'll never get through it, you understand me?"

Matthew lifted his head slowly, eyeing Holden. "Yeah. I understand."

"No more smashing glass or swinging shotguns around like a lunatic, then."

Matthew nodded. "What the hell do you suggest I do instead?"

"Wait," Holden said. "Your father has Waterman

and Grayhawk turning over every rock. The FBI is going to be getting involved, as well. There's not a damn thing any of us can do beyond what's already being done. At least not until the kidnappers make contact again to set up an exchange.''

Matthew looked toward his father. Ryan nodded. ''He's right, son. I know it's hard to take, but Holden is absolutely right.''

Finally, with a sigh, Matthew nodded. ''Jeez, I'm dizzy. What the hell did Lucinda give me?''

''She didn't say,'' Holden told him. ''I'll ask her when I see her.''

Matthew's brows went up. ''You're seeing her?''

''You got a problem with that, cousin?''

Matthew shook his head. ''If she's smart, she'll get as far away from the Fortunes as she can. You included.''

''Well, let's hope she's not quite as smart as she seems, then.'' Holden turned to Ryan. ''Is there anything more I can do here?''

Ryan shook his head. ''You've been a great deal of help today, Holden. Sometimes...sometimes I think you take after your mother far more than you do your father. And when you do, I'm glad of it.''

''I'll drive Mother home, then.''

''I think she plans to say here tonight,'' Lily said.

''Fine. If you need me, call the house. If I'm out, leave a message. I'll check in often.''

Ryan nodded, and Holden left.

Getting into his car, he pulled out of the drive, and headed straight into Red Rock. Red Rock General Hospital was only a few minutes away, and that was where he was bound. Because until he followed this insane idea that he'd come up with earlier to its conclusion…it wasn't going to leave him alone.

Lucinda was running, the newborn cradled in her arms. The tiny bit of a thing fit in the palms of her hands easily. Three pounds, two ounces. The nurses were running beside her, the baby's father bringing up the rear. There had been no time to prepare, no warning. The girl had been giving birth even as Lucinda arrived. Before any background information could be obtained.

The neonatal resident, Dr. Edward Greene, came running from the other direction.

"Condition?" he shouted.

"Critical. She's barely breathing!"

Greene took the baby from Lucinda's arms like the second runner in a relay race. He turned and raced up the hall toward the neonatal intensive care unit. Lucinda stood there and watched him go. The adrenaline in her blood dropped drastically, and she braced her arms against the nearest wall, nearly sagging to the floor. Holding back the tears was choking her. She wasn't supposed to get this involved… Wasn't supposed to feel this strongly—

"Hey…hey, hold on…"

A pair of strong hands clasped her waist from behind. Holden Fortune's voice surrounded her. She managed to stiffen her knees, stand up straight, swallow the tears, and turn to face him.

"Jeez, you look awful."

"That baby looked worse. Did you see…?"

Holden nodded, sending a grim glance in the direction Dr. Greene had run with the child. "Will it live?"

Lucinda shook her head. "I don't know."

Holden looked down into her eyes. "What happened?"

There were shouts and crying from a room a few doors down, and Lucinda blinked herself back to reality. "Can I tell you about it later? I need to talk to the mother right now."

"Not a job I imagine you're looking forward to."

"No. It's not."

"I'll be here when you come out," he said.

Now why should those words give her a surge of comfort? She wasn't sure. She only knew that knowing he would be there after this ordeal, knowing someone would be there, made her feel just a tiny bit better.

Holden watched Lucy's face across the table in the hospital cafeteria as she sipped stale coffee and poured her stress out. She cared. Doctors weren't supposed to, he thought, at least not to this degree, but he didn't think she could help herself.

"Premature," she was saying. "At least nine weeks, maybe more. And his mother never saw a doctor until she was in the final stages of labor. The baby was crowning when I got to her. No neonatal specialist in sight. We had to call Greene in from home, and even then he was almost too late."

Holden nodded, saying nothing. Just letting her talk it out.

"The baby didn't breathe. We had to bag her to get her started, and then she was barely getting enough oxygen into her bloodstream to keep her lips from turning blue. Their lungs aren't fully developed at this stage. If the mother had come in earlier, we could have given her a shot to help that along, maybe even stopped the labor altogether.''

''So why didn't she?''

Lucy closed her eyes. ''She figured the less time she spent here, the less it would cost her.'' She sighed. ''She started screaming when she saw that baby, so tiny, so limp, and just as blue as... She kept saying she'd have come sooner if she'd known... See, that's just it. A lot of these women don't know. They don't know the first thing about prenatal care and the risks they're running by not getting it. They need educa-tion...and once they have it, they need a place to go where they can get the care they need at low or no cost. Otherwise, the education will be useless.''

Holden nodded, seeing now why this clinic idea of hers meant so much to her. ''You've had one hell of a day of it today, haven't you, Lucy?''

She met his eyes. ''I'm probably boring you to tears with all this. And it's not as if you haven't had a hellish day yourself.''

''I don't think you could bore me if you tried. But I do think we could both use a little diversion.''

She narrowed her eyes. ''Such as?''

''A movie? You name it.''

She lowered her head. ''I'm too exhausted for that.''

''Well, you have to eat, don't you?''

She nodded, sighing, knowing this was a bad idea.

''Don't tell me you intend to do it here.'' Holden glanced down at his cup. ''Judging by their coffee, I'd say that would be a bad decision.'' He sucked in a breath. ''We could, uh, go to my place.''

Stands to reason it would bother you to hang out in the lap of luxury while your patients can't even afford their prenatal vitamins. And I don't want you all tense and guilty. I want you to relax."

He took a seat beside her and gave the swing a push with his feet. Lucinda leaned back against the plush cushions, her aching head pillowed by softness. In the distance, lush green hills and occasional clusters of woods unrolled as far as the eye could see. Dark shapes dotted the nighttime landscape here and there. And way off on the horizon she could see the hazy outline and lighted windows of the Double Crown, about two miles distant.

"This is a peaceful place," she said.

"Yes. It's my favorite spot on the entire spread."

"Really? Even at 3:00 a.m.?"

He nodded. "Especially at 3:00 a.m. Listen."

Lucinda let her eyes fall closed, let the breeze caress her into a state of calm she hadn't felt in weeks, and listened. The gentle laughter of a stream not too far off. The call of a night bird to punctuate the unending whir of crickets and tree frogs. A bullfrog sang his deep baritone chorus. The wind made the leaves dance in the trees.

"Heaven," she whispered.

"Yeah," he replied.

They never did eat.

Holden woke to softness and a scent he found intensely arousing. Within a moment of opening his eyes he identified it. It was Lucy. Her hair, her skin... something. They'd fallen asleep on the porch swing. And now she was curled up in his arms with her head on his shoulder, hugging his waist like a lover.

He stared down at her, wondering if he had ever in his life spent the night with a woman and not had sex with her.

Nope, he didn't think so.

About that time Lucy's head lifted until her eyes locked with his. She blinked, and those eyes got as big as saucers. She was just so damned cute in the morning. Hair all tossed around, eyes so big and confused and unfocused. Her arms were still locked around his waist. His held her tightly to him. And he supposed he must not be fully awake himself, because he suddenly moved the merest bit it took to settle his mouth atop hers.

Damn, that was good. He tilted her head and kissed her deeper, one hand creeping over her nape and into her hair until it cupped her head so he could move her into just the right position. He heard the soft sigh that stuttered out of her. He tasted it. And then he pulled her right into his lap, bending over her to kiss the living hell out of her.

That was the wrong thing to do. She went stiff. Her hands flattened to his chest, and she shoved for all she was worth.

Holden lifted his head, opened his eyes. Hers were wide open and glittering up at him. "Get off me," was all she said.

He didn't bother telling her that she was the one sitting on his lap. Instead he straightened, letting her slide off him. Not to sit beside him, but landing on her feet on the redwood floor instead. She smoothed her hair, narrowed her eyes. "Just so we're clear on this," she said, "I don't do one-night stands anymore."

He lifted his brows. "Does that mean you did once?"

Her look turned thunderous.

"Forget I asked that. It was rude...unforgivable. Look, I didn't mean to kiss you like that just now."

"You didn't?" she asked, sarcasm dripping from her voice.

"No," he said, looking at his feet, going for humble and apologetic. "I opened my eyes and there you were, snuggled up in my arms. So close, so soft and...and so beautiful." He peeked up at her. The anger was fading. Disbelief remained, but she didn't look ready to skin him now. At least, not as much as she had a moment ago. "I thought maybe I was dreaming," he went on. "And when you kissed me back, I knew I didn't want to wake up."

Lucy stared hard at him, searched his eyes, sought the lie, but he was too good to reveal it. Finally she sighed and shook her head. He did have one thing on her. She had kissed him back. At first.

And it had been like touching some unknown element and watching it shimmer and ripple in reaction to that touch.

Wow. Why the hell did Lucy Brightwater have to be a good girl?

"Just don't let it happen again." She straightened her skirt, smoothed her hair again. "I—I should go."

"No, wait." For some reason he didn't want her to leave just yet. Something about it felt wrong. He was almost desperate—very unlike him—but he couldn't help that. "We never ate last night...and...man, do you smell that?"

She sniffed. She smelled it, he could tell she did. Consuella must be whipping up one hell of a Sunday breakfast this morning.

"I'm really not hungry," Lucy said. Then her stomach growled.

Holden looked down at her belly and crooked a brow. "Oh, yeah?"

"Yeah," she said.

"Well, I have plans for the day, and I'm going to bug you until you cooperate with them, so you may as well eat first."

"What sort of plans?"

"You'll just have to wait and see."

"I'm on call—"

"Liar. I checked, and you're free."

"But...I need to check on Claudia."

"Already on the itinerary."

Lucy frowned hard at him, falling silent. "Just what do you want from me, Holden Fortune?"

"You really want to know?" he asked.

"Yes, I really want to know. Why all this attention? Why are you making such an effort?"

He pursed his lips, took a breath. "Actually," he said, "I think I might just want to marry you."

Lucy's jaw dropped open and she stared up at him in abject shock. When she didn't speak, it was, he assumed, because she couldn't. He took advantage of that situation, taking her by the arm and guiding her back into the house, as she shuffled at his side, just gaping at him. And by the time she recovered the ability to speak, Holden was pushing her chair underneath her in the breakfast room, and unfolding her napkin on her lap for her.

"Coffee or tea?" he asked, reaching for her cup.

"What the hell do you mean, you want to marry me?" she replied.

Consuella stood halfway from the kitchen door to the breakfast table, a tray of pastries in her hand, and said, "¡Dios mío!"

Four

Lucinda was still digesting what he'd just blurted to her. Only now she was sitting in a charming little breakfast nook, in a sunroom, with glass walls and ceiling in a curving pattern that drenched her in cheerful yellow sunlight. In front of her was a heaping plate, a brimming coffee cup, and a juice glass full of liquid sunshine, apparently, just in case there wasn't enough of the other kind.

"Good God, I can't eat all this."

The maid, or cook or whoever, Consuella, a plump middle-aged woman who seemed to be practically beaming, swooped in and snatched her plate away, replacing it with a fresh one. "I get you whatever you wish for, *chiquita*. You want fruit? Eh? Yogurt? Oh, Consuella's special omelette, eh? I make—"

"No, no, please." Lucinda held up a hand. "Don't go to any trouble. I just meant there was too much of this wonderful food on my plate, is all…"

"Psssh, it is no trouble at all, Miss Lucinda. No trouble at all for Mister Holden's bride-to-be!" She clapped her hands together, grinning ear to ear. "Such a nice girl, too!" she bubbled as she trotted back through the door into the kitchen.

"But I'm not…" Lucinda drew a breath through gritted teeth and glared at Holden. "What would possess you to say such a thing where she could hear?'' she asked.

"To be honest, I didn't realize she was there when I—"

"She thinks you were serious for goodness' sake!"

"Well I..." Holden licked his lips, buttered a blueberry muffin, and set his knife down precisely. "I was serious."

Lucy blinked. "You...you've only known me for approximately twenty-four hours."

"What're you, kidding? I've known you since high school."

"You don't even remember me from high school."

He averted his eyes. "I do so."

"Oh, yeah?"

"Yeah."

"Prove it, then. What do you remember?"

He took a deep breath, knitting his brow. "I remember you were always around. I used to wonder if you were following me, but I kind of thought you were too shy for that. You never said much. Just seemed to be off in the distance...watching me whenever I looked up. At football practice, or at lunch or whenever."

Licking her lips, Lucinda reached for a muffin and tore a chunk out of it, wishing it were Holden Fortune's flesh. God, how she'd ached for him, longed for him, fantasized about him.... Reality hadn't been half as good as the dream, though.

"You must have really liked me, didn't you?"

She eyed him, saying nothing.

"So it stands to reason you could like me again."

He sighed. "You got me out of a mess once, I remember that."

She'd been bringing the muffin to her lips, but stopped halfway. "Oh?"

"It was the Valentine's Day dance, senior year. I was going with some blonde...what the hell was her name?"

"Tiffany," Lucinda said. "Her name was Tiffany."

"Right. Right, Tiffany." He grinned and shook his head. "She dumped me that night."

"And you were devastated?"

"Yeah. Well, no girl had ever dumped me before. Wrecked my perfect record, you know. Made me look bad in front of the guys."

Lucinda lifted her brows.

"Someone had smuggled some booze into the dance, and I got into it. Wound up so drunk I could barely stand up. And then I danced with you."

She nodded. "To make Tiffany jealous."

He looked at her sharply. "Well, that wasn't the only reason."

"No, I didn't think so, either, at first. In fact, you were so cuddly and clingy, I thought...well, it only took a few steps before I realized you were holding me so close because you'd fall down if you didn't."

Holden's brows furrowed. "Hey, that's not fair. How do you know I wasn't holding you because I wanted to?"

"How do you think I know?"

He scowled even more deeply, trying to remember. "One of the chaperones smelled the booze on my breath, threatened to call my father, but you stepped in and said you'd drive me home safe and sound. Got me out of it. They never called Cameron, and I never got my hide tanned. Not only that, but I made it home in one piece. All thanks to you.''

She nodded, forcing a sweet smile. ''And when we got back to your place?''

Holden blinked, his gaze turning inward. ''I must have passed out. I don't remember a damn thing.''

''No. No, I know you don't. Do you remember that you were back with Tiffany the very next day?''

He stared hard at her. ''My God...it never occurred to me to think...that hurt you, didn't it? I can't believe it.''

She blinked and turned her head. ''Don't be ridiculous.''

''If I was back with Tiffany the next day, Lucy, then the only thing that proves is that I was a damn idiot who didn't know a good thing when I saw it.''

''Yeah, right. Look, I really have to leave.'' She pushed her chair away from the table, got to her feet.

He was out of his chair in a heartbeat, gripping her shoulders. ''It seems a little odd you'd have been that upset over it, though. I mean, it was only one dance, after all, and I was drunk, and...'' He frowned. ''Did something else happen between us that night?''

She looked away. ''Don't you think you'd remember if it did?''

Holden searched her face for a long time, then finally licked his lips and sighed. ''Look, can we just forget about all of that? Please? I was a kid, spoiled, stupid, self-centered and drunk to boot. And besides, what I'm offering you now has nothing to do with that.''

''Doesn't it?''

"No."

She nodded, staring him down, unblinking. "And just what are you offering me, Holden?"

He blew a long sigh through pursed lips. "You ought to know. You're the one who put the idea into my head." He waited. She said nothing. He let go of her arms, and paced away. "A deal. An agreement. An...an arrangement."

She blinked slowly, and finally felt as if she had a clue where he was taking this.

"You marry me, be my wife for a year. I inherit my share of dear old Dad's fortune, and you get your clinic. We both walk away at the end of twelve months with exactly what we want."

"Do you realize how much money it will take to make the clinic a reality?"

He turned and smiled a little crookedly. "I expected a flat-out no. This is progress."

"I need a million dollars, Holden."

"I'll give it to you. More if you want. Whatever you need."

Lucinda's throat went as dry as desert sand. "You'd give me...a million dollars?"

"I'll be inheriting hundreds of millions. But I can't get a nickel of it until I am married to a respectable woman."

Lucinda sank back into her chair as all the will fled her body. She could see it all. The clinic, the educational programs... My God, with a million she could even buy a couple of small buses to transport women to and from their appointments....

"I couldn't... It's ridiculous."

"Why? What's so ridiculous about it? I like you,

Lucy. You're smart, and capable and strong. Hell, how can you turn it down when it's the perfect answer to your problems?''

She blinked again. "A—a business arrangement." He nodded. "It would... I mean, it wouldn't change anything. It would just be on paper, this marriage." She almost bit her tongue trying to stop the words from coming.

Holden walked slowly back to his own chair, sat and studied his plate. "Actually it would have to be slightly more than that."

Frowning, Lucinda lifted her head.

"Well, it would have to look real. I mean, if my father's lawyers aren't convinced...and as for the rest of the family..."

"What about them?"

"They'd crucify me if they thought I was just...using you."

She nodded slowly. "So I'd have to move in here. Not that I'm actually considering this, but—"

"Here, or the apartment," he said quickly.

She lifted one brow, glared at him.

"Right," he told her, "you'd have to move in here. I've got a whole wing to myself, though. You could have your own space. All you want, in fact. My mother would love having you here. And you'd have servants, and the pool, that back porch swing whenever you want it. A car to drive that doesn't stall out at red lights."

"My car does not stall out at red lights." She sighed and nodded slowly. "But just for the record, between us...nothing would have to...happen."

Holden studied her face. "No. Absolutely not. In fact, I'd prefer it didn't."

She felt her brows raise. "Gee, thanks."

"Come on, Lucy. You know damn good and well you're a knockout. I just think...this would be better for both of us if we kept it...cool."

She drew a breath, sighed heavily. "I can't. It's quite an offer, Holden, but I—"

"Think about it?"

She fell silent again. This was stupid. She couldn't possibly... "Okay. I'll think about it. Give me a couple of days. All right?"

He met her eyes, held them. "I can't ask for more than that, can I?"

She had to be out of her mind. Completely out of her mind to actually be considering this.

But she was considering it. And the more she thought on it, the better it looked. Hell, it wasn't as if she'd be giving anything up. And in a year she could have her clinic.

She'd gone back to her own apartment to shower and change clothes. Holden planned to pick her up there in time for lunch. Apparently, he was serious about all of this. Serious enough to want to spend time with her today, probably in an effort to convince her to accept his deal. And she was too damned weak where he was concerned to tell him no.

But there was a certain poetic irony to all of this. After he'd all but demolished her life, he was now back offering her one of her longtime dreams on a silver platter. Her clinic.

But what about her other dream? The baby she so

wanted. Could she have both? Could she put off having a child until this…this arrangement with Holden was over? She certainly couldn't do both at once. He'd made it pretty clear this was to be a hands-off arrangement. Well, she supposed she'd have the answer to that question today. When she got the results of her ultrasound exam, she'd know whether putting off having a child for another year was a viable option.

And there was another worry that kept haunting her mind. Try as she might to forget them, Lily's words kept floating back to her. Holden Fortune could hurt her if she let him. And she was damned afraid she could let him, all too easily. There was still something inside her…some feelings lingering there, left over from high school, she supposed. That childhood crush, that first case of puppy love had left remnants. Or were they scars? And why was it she still felt like a clumsy, skinny teenager when she was around Holden Fortune?

Her doorbell chimed before she even finished drying her hair. She'd pulled on jeans and her favorite white T-shirt with the cat decal. Her feet were still bare, her hair still damp. Great. Well, he might as well get a good look at what he was getting here. And she supposed she couldn't look much worse than she had this morning, waking in his arms still wearing the clothes she'd slept in.

She opened the door.

Holden smiled at her. "I know, I'm early. Sorry."

"It's okay. Come on in." He did, and looked around. Her cat, Cleo, eighteen pounds and about as graceful as a moose, stomped over to him, stared up for a second or two, and then rubbed against his legs.

Holden bent to scratch Cleo's head. "Wow. That's some cat."

"You allergic or anything?"

"Not that I know of. Although if I were, I suppose we'd know soon enough. I've never seen so much hair on one animal."

"He's a Persian," she said. "They have a lot of fur. And it isn't the hair that causes allergic reactions, anyway, it's the dander. But if you're not careful..." He'd scooped the cat into his arms and straightened with a grunt before she finished. Lucinda licked her lips. "If you're not careful, that fur will be all over your clothes," she finished.

"You're one heavy fellow, you know that? What do you eat, sides of beef? Hmm?"

Lucinda watched him. He didn't drop the cat and start brushing stray hairs from his shirt, or wrinkle his nose in distaste or start sneezing, the way her last three dates had each done, respectively. He just kept petting the cat, who began purring so loudly it sounded like a B-52 was dive-bombing her living room.

"What's his name?"

"Cleo," she said. And when she said his name, her pet looked toward her.

"Poor thing's obviously underfed," Holden said. He stopped petting, and Cleo immediately batted his hand. "Oooh, bossy little cuss, aren't you?"

Lucinda took Cleo from his arms and put him down, and Cleo gave her a disgusted look before padding away. Then she looked back at Holden. "So, you don't hate my cat?"

"No. Was I supposed to?"

"Where I go, he goes. You ought to know that."

Holden smiled. "Oh, man, my mother is going to—"

"I hadn't thought of that," she interrupted. Then she paced away, hand on her chin. "She'll probably hate him. All the cat hair on that expensive furniture of hers. And he's going to be all over that house. We'll never keep him quarantined in one wing."

"Lucy, will you slow down? I was going to say, my mother will be in seventh heaven. Dad would never let her keep pets in the house, and she always wanted to. She and Cleo will be best friends, I guarantee it."

"Oh." She lowered her head.

"Thought you'd found a reason to turn me down, didn't you?"

"Oh, don't worry. There are others." She looked up, saw the disappointment in his face, felt guilty.

"Should we discuss them now, then? Because I'll tell you, Lucy, I'm willing to do anything to make this work. It's the perfect solution to both our problems, and the more I think about it, the better it sounds."

She closed her eyes, exhaled slowly. "No. Look, I've barely had three hours to think about this. I just need time to work it all out in my mind, okay?"

"So, I should stop pressing."

She nodded.

"And I shouldn't have shown up early."

"No," she said. "You shouldn't. You can see I'm not ready."

He looked her over, from her head to her toes, and then he smiled. "You're barefoot," he observed. "You have cute feet."

"Flattery isn't going to convince me, either."

He gave his head a shake and met her eyes again. "Look, I was going to go over to the main house to check on Matthew and Claudia, and I thought you might want to come along. Do you?"

"Yes, very much."

"Good. And, um…that wasn't flattery. You really do have cute feet."

"Right. I think I'll put some shoes on, anyway, if it's all the same to you. And I need to be back here by three. I have an, uh, appointment."

Holden frowned. "A date?"

"Of course not. I need to see someone at the hospital. It won't take long."

"So then, you'll be free for dinner afterward?"

She sighed. "I'll let you know."

"Good enough." He settled into a chair, and Cleo was on his lap a second later. "So, go finish getting ready," he said, stroking the cat and looking perfectly content to sit and wait.

Holden had certainly put on a good show. Ever the gentleman, anyone would think he was just the opposite of the man she knew him to be. An uncaring womanizer. Instead he seemed friendly, attentive, even kind. His concern for his family…well, that part was real. She had, she realized in surprise, actually enjoyed the time she'd spent with him today. And she adored his mother, Mary Ellen. The woman was everything Lucinda had ever wanted to be. Strong, sure of herself, graceful.

At her doctor's appointment that afternoon, though, all of those thoughts fled her mind, replaced by one new revelation. One she'd hoped and prayed she would never have to face.

Lucinda sat very still, absorbing the blow. "You're absolutely sure the ovary is going to have to come out."

"I'm afraid so," Karen Flemming replied. "Look, it can wait...a few months, maybe even a year, but not a minute longer. It's going to have to go, and I wouldn't push it any further." She shook her head slowly. "You've seen the test results. You can interpret them as well as I can."

"Yeah." Lucinda eyed the detestable manila folder and tried to blink back tears.

"It's for your own health," Karen went on. "Precancerous cysts are bad in and of themselves, but with your family history...."

"I know. My mother died of ovarian cancer. I'm a doctor, Karen, I know what that means as well as you do."

Karen nodded slowly. "I know how desperately you want a baby, Lucinda. I suppose if you were to get pregnant right away..."

"Oh, come on, Karen, stop talking to me like I'm a layman. We both know that I only have one ovary, and that cuts my chances of conceiving a child in two. It could take me months to get pregnant, even if I could find a willing man to help out."

Karen lowered her head. "There's artificial insemination. You don't need to wait for a man to start trying. Like you said, you know what you're looking at here just as well as I do. And I think you also know what advice you would give to one of your patients in this same situation. Don't you?"

Lucinda looked up slowly. "Yes. I'd tell them to have the ovary removed right away. I'd tell them that to wait too long would be taking an unnecessary risk. I'd tell them to adopt." She lowered her head. "But, unfortunately, I'm not smart enough to take my own advice."

"Then what are you going to do?"

Lucinda lifted her chin. "I'm going to get pregnant just as soon as possible. Because the longer I wait, the less chance I'll have of ever...having a child."

Karen nodded. "I'm sorry. I wish the news had been better."

"So do I," Lucinda said, and she got up from the chair. She was already dressed. She picked up her bag, and turned toward the door.

"Look, if you want to talk about this some more..."

"Yeah. I know. Thanks, Karen."

Karen nodded, one hand on Lucinda's shoulder in a reassuring squeeze. She sighed, turned and left the office, stepping into the hospital corridor, responding automatically to the greetings of co-workers as they passed.

Well, this was it, then. Time was running out for her. She needed to conceive a child now. Right away. And the answer...the answer was sitting at home waiting for her call. A man who wanted to marry her for a year. Long enough. It would be long enough.

It's wrong, some part of her whispered. Wrong to try to use Holden to get pregnant, without even telling him.

And yet, was it really so wrong? If it hadn't been for Holden Fortune and that one-night stand so long ago, she would have two functioning ovaries, not one.

She could have one removed and still retain a chance at motherhood one day. But now...

She stepped into her office, and sank into her chair. She didn't want to remember, but the memories came anyway. The sudden pains that had left her breathless on the floor. The bleeding that seemed as if it would never stop. The mad rush to the hospital, and the chaos in the ER. And then, waking later from the surgery as a soft-spoken doctor told her what had happened to her.

All because of Holden's drunken attempt to make his girlfriend jealous.

If she didn't do something, and soon, she would never have the chance to have a child.

He was attracted to her. She was fairly certain of that. His kiss this morning... Something tingled up her nape and she closed her eyes against it. He was attracted to her. That was all she needed to know. And even though he'd said this...this arrangement would be strictly "hands off," she knew she could make it otherwise.

Hell, all she'd have to do would be to get him drunk. It had worked once, hadn't it? It would be poetic justice.

She clamped down her conscience and reached for her telephone, punching in Holden's number. He picked up on the second ring. "So," she said without preamble, "are we still on for dinner tonight?"

She could almost hear his smile coming through the line. "You bet we are," he said. "I'll pick you up in an hour."

"I'll be waiting."

Five

Lucy was nervous, fidgeting, and drop-dead gorgeous tonight. Holden studied her across the table, candle-light dancing on her face, in her eyes, and he won-dered if maybe he had other reasons for choosing her to be his wife. She'd been handy, yes. She'd been in need of something he could give, and, he thought, willing to agree, true enough. But there was more... he was drawn to the woman. He had always been drawn to her. Before, he'd given himself a million reasons to stay away from her. And now it seemed like he was busily concocting just as many reasons why all those reasons no longer applied. First, he'd justified his in-terest by telling himself she was no longer young and vulnerable and nursing a crush on him. Then he'd de-cided it would be all right because he'd keep this on the level of a business arrangement, that no feelings would be involved.

But to tell the truth, he was looking forward to being in close proximity to her for the next year or so.

That worried him, though he couldn't have said why.

She'd barely touched her food.

"Are you going to keep me in suspense all night, Lucy?"

She looked up from what had appeared to be an

intense study of the glazed asparagus on her plate. "What?"

"I get the feeling you've reached a decision. So, will you tell me what it is?"

She blinked, averted her eyes. "There are...a couple of things I want to say first."

"Okay." Holden leaned back in his chair, picked up his wineglass, sipped. And watched her. She had such incredible skin. Like satin, coppery and smooth. The candlelight caressed it and danced on it like a kiss.

She drew a breath. "I'm not as well-known as you, Holden, but I do have a career, a reputation to think about."

He nodded. "A very good reputation, as I understand it."

"So I wouldn't want it destroyed. I think you know what I'm talking about."

He sat up a little, totally lost. "I'm afraid I don't."

With a sigh, she took a swallow from her own wineglass. Then dabbed her lips with the napkin. "If we were married and you continued bedding a different woman every night of the week, I—"

He held up a hand, stopping her. "Okay. Now I see. You'd want me to be...faithful."

She nodded. "Or at least...discreet."

Holden lifted his brows. "Discreet. You mean, you wouldn't mind my sleeping around as long as it was kept quiet?" He shook his head. "I don't quite swallow that, Doc. But it's best we put our cards on the table here and now. Which is it you want? Faithful or discreet?"

She swallowed hard. "Faithful." She looked away when she said it.

She was amusing to watch when she was embarrassed. He liked the way the color stained her cheeks, the way her eyes danced away from his when he tried to look too deeply. "I can handle that," he said, speaking slow, watching those eyes. "But I have one concern you probably ought to be aware of."

"And that is?"

"It would have to go both ways, Lucy. If there's anyone you're sleeping with, then you're going to have to end it."

Her eyes widened this time before she looked away.

Holden tossed his napkin on the table and got up. He crossed to her and held out a hand. "Let's dance while we talk, hmm?"

Licking her lips and lifting her chin like a martyr going to the stake, she took his hand, and Holden pulled her into his arms. She was soft against him. Soft, and small, and he liked that.

As he swept her onto the floor, moving slowly, savoring the feel of her perhaps a bit more than was wise, he went on. "The thing is, I like sex. I enjoy it. I'm not addicted to it or anything, but a year of celibacy is going to be a challenge. Still…I can stick to my promise if you can. And if it becomes a problem, I'll say so. And I'll expect you to do the same."

Her voice very soft, very hoarse, she replied, "You mean…if one of us were to decide we wanted to…"

He stopped dancing. Just stood still on the floor, holding her against him, her head on his shoulder. She'd had a couple glasses of wine with dinner. Maybe she got drunk easily. Maybe she was saying things she didn't mean. But damn, his reaction to his interpretation of those words was almost violent.

He hadn't realized until that very moment how much he wanted her.

"Have you?"

She said nothing. Holden stepped back just slightly, enough so he could cup her chin and turn her face up to his. Red. She was beet-red.

"No, of course not. I don't want you to think I'm willing to...to sell myself, sexually, for the sake of this clinic. I'm not."

"I don't think that. I know better than that, Lucy."

She closed her eyes, maybe about to give up on the subject. So Holden decided to help her along. Because if she wanted more than a business arrangement out of this deal then he was going to have to withdraw the offer.

"There is a certain attraction between us. You've been aware of that, too, haven't you?" he asked her.

"You...are attracted to me?"

He smiled just slightly. "Don't tell me you didn't know? Yeah, Doc. I'm attracted to you." He took a breath and sighed. "I'm pretty intensely attracted to you."

"Oh."

He pulled her closer again, resumed dancing. "So, does knowing that make this easier or harder?" he asked.

"Easier...I guess."

"Then is it safe to assume you're attracted to me, too?"

A soft sigh wafted over the sensitive skin of his neck and he involuntarily shivered in pleasure. Damn.

"I pretty much always have been."

"So it's good that we get this out of the way, up

front. What we intend to do—and more importantly, *not* to do—about this attraction.''

"I suppose it is."

"We can't act on it, Lucy."

She stiffened just slightly.

"It would mess everything up. This is strictly business between you and me. And, hell, I think we both know it's only a chemical thing, anyway. I'm the last kind of man you'd ever want to get involved with. And you... You're the furthest thing from what I'd call my type."

He felt her head nod against his shoulder. "Yes, I suppose that's all true."

"So, can you live with that kind of arrangement? A year of celibacy?''

"It only seems fair," she said quickly. "I mean, if you can handle it, I certainly can."

Staring down into those black eyes, he suddenly wasn't so sure all of this would be as easy as he thought it would. God, he had visions of her naked and willing in his mind already.

"I'll do it, then," she told him. "I'll marry you."

He wondered why he was suddenly smiling so broadly when he'd only just decided this might not be such a great idea. "When? Pick a date and I'm there. Any kind of wedding you want, the biggest blowout Texas has ever seen if you—"

"No," she said. She settled her head against his shoulder again and nudged him into motion. "No, nothing like that. Your family is in no state to be worrying about some big event. Besides, I don't want to wait that long.''

Holden closed his eyes in abject agony. "No," he whispered. "No, neither do I."

"Couldn't we just go to city hall or something?" she asked.

"Yes." He spread his palms on her back, let her body heat warm them, lowered his head so he could inhale the fragrance of her hair.

"We can do the blood test right at the hospital tomorrow morning. Have the results back in an hour. Then we can get the license. Everything could be ready before noon."

"Absolutely," he said.

"Will that give you time to see your lawyer, get the prenup ready and everything?"

Holden frowned, and again stopped dancing. What was it about her that could make him forget something so vital, so obvious? Without a prenup she could serve twelve months as his wife and walk away with everything he had when it was over. God, hadn't he learned a thing from his uncle Ryan's unfortunate marriage to Sophia Barnes?

Then again, Lucy was nothing like Sophia. Not even close.

He blinked down at Lucy, not quite sure he had realized before the full extent of her...her goodness. He wouldn't ruin her the way his father had ruined his mother. He wouldn't let himself do that. "I think it will be plenty of time," he said. "For what I'm paying my lawyer, he can take care of this on short notice."

She nodded. "We'll need witnesses."

"I'll handle it."

Drawing a breath, she nodded hard. "Tomorrow afternoon, then? Say, three o'clock, at city hall?"

He nodded. "I'll be there."

Her smile was shaky, her eyes, never looking head-on into his. The warning bells in his head were getting louder all the time. What the hell had changed between this afternoon and tonight?

He leaned down, and pressed his lips to her forehead to seal the deal. Her tense body relaxed just a little, but he didn't push his luck. When he lifted his head again, her eyes seemed misty, though it was dim and hard to tell.

All of this change had occurred between the time he'd left her this afternoon and picked her up tonight. Hadn't she said she had some kind of appointment today? At the hospital?

"Holden?"

He snapped to attention, looked down at her.

"There's...there's one more thing you need to know."

"Is there?"

"Yes. No matter what else happens between us in the next twelve months...I'm...I'm not going to fall in love with you."

"You're not?"

"No. That's what you're worried about here, isn't it? That I'll start feeling something for you, wanting more than you're capable of giving? But I'm not a little girl anymore, and my sense of self-preservation is too strong to let me do anything that destructive. So, I won't be falling in love with you. You don't need to worry about that."

He nodded. "Good, Lucy. I'm glad we understand each other."

She sighed, and seemed to feel better about things.

And Holden thought about what she'd said. *I'm not going to fall in love with you.* And already, something in his heart was telling him he'd never be able to say the same.

Lucinda was rigid and stiff. She was only doing what she had to do, and nice girls finished last, so it was time to don her Leona hat and quit being a wimp. Waiting around for the right man. Waiting and hoping and getting older by the day while her one remaining ovary slowly declared war on her body, and her biological clock ticked down to Ground Zero.

Well, she was done waiting.

She stood in the city hall building in front of Judge Will Schapiro, who'd been perfectly willing to shuffle his schedule to accommodate Holden's request. Although Holden, apparently, wasn't quite as generous. He hadn't shown up yet.

"Good to meet you, Dr. Brightwater," the judge said, rising, coming around the desk to take her hand briefly. "Just have a seat, make yourself comfortable. Holden should be along any minute now."

He was a jolly man, hardly looked the part of his "hanging judge" reputation. His plump face, nearly bald head with its whisker-thin coat of white fuzz, and soft blue eyes made him look more like a friendly town minister than a tough-as-nails judge.

She sat in the leather chair in front of his desk as he eyed her. Lucinda got the feeling she was being inspected in some kind of wonder. She wore an off-white skirt with a sleeveless satin blouse of ivory. Her hair was caught up in back, with tendrils framing her face. Pearl drop earrings dangled, cool against her neck. She wore makeup, which was not her usual custom. But she'd wanted to look good today.

"I can hardly believe that old boy is finally settling down," Judge Schapiro said, settling into the seat beside hers rather than returning to the one behind his desk. "Tell me, Dr. Brightwater, how did you manage to rope the wildest bronc in Texas?"

She smiled slightly, though his words made her stomach clench. "Now, now, Your Honor. How do you know he isn't the one who roped me?"

He slapped his thigh, laughing out loud. "Well, if he did, then he's a lucky man. I like you, young lady. You take my advice and keep a tight rein on that one. He's had his head for far too long already."

"I'll do that."

There was a commotion just beyond the doors, and then they opened and three people spilled through them, talking all at once. But Lucinda only saw Holden. He took her breath away. His tanned good looks accented the dark suit and snow-white shirt underneath. He seemed broader in the shoulders, dressed this way. It pleased her to think he'd taken pains to look the part of eager groom. Even while the thought of trying to seduce him scared her to death.

"Lucy," he said, coming forward to take both her hands, drawing her close for a brief, brotherly kiss. "I'm sorry I'm late. I had trouble digging up a second witness."

She managed to look past him to where his brother Logan stood, clearly stunned and confused. Beside him was a young woman Lucinda had seen at the ill-fated christening party. She had pretty brown hair pulled back in a no-nonsense bun, and huge brown eyes behind a pair of gold wire-rimmed glasses.

"Lucy, you know my brother Logan?" Holden asked.

Lucinda nodded toward Logan. "Thanks so much for coming," she said.

"I don't know you very well, Lucinda, but I have to tell you I think you're making a hell of a mistake here."

Lucinda felt her eyes widen. The other woman gasped out loud, and Holden shot his brother a glare that would have wilted lettuce.

"I'm sorry, Holden, but I have to say it. This is coming out of nowhere, and we both know you have motives she knows nothing about. Lucinda, are you sure you're aware of what you're getting into?"

Holden gripped his brother's arm. "Maybe we'd better have a talk outside, little brother."

"Holden, no." Lucinda made her voice as calm as she could manage. "Logan, I appreciate your concern. I do. But your brother has been very honest with me about his...situation, as well as his motives. And I assure you, I'm not some bubble-headed twit who would make a decision like this without giving it serious thought."

"Yeah? Well, neither was my mother. But she spent the next several decades paying for it all the same."

"Logan, maybe you should let Dr. Brightwater make her own decisions," the woman said, her voice soft, her brown eyes on Logan's face.

Logan sighed, and glanced down at Holden's hand on his arm. Holden let go.

"Some wedding day these two are giving you, isn't

it?'' the woman asked, dragging her gaze from Logan's and offering a hand to Lucinda. ''I'm Emily Applegate, Logan's assistant at the Fortune TX offices.''

''And the only poor soul they could drag away on such short notice to be our second witness, I would guess,'' Lucinda said, taking the woman's hand.

''I'm glad to do it,'' she replied.

Lucinda could see that she was. In fact, from the way she looked at her boss, Lucinda guessed Emily would likely be glad to do just about anything he asked of her.

The judge cleared his throat, and all four heads turned in his direction. ''If you're ready to proceed?''

Lucinda blinked in surprise as Holden's hand closed around hers. She was scared, trembling a bit, and completely unsure that rushing headlong into this marriage was the right thing to do. The thing was, it was the *only* thing to do right now. It made perfect sense, didn't it?

''You ready, Lucy?''

She glanced up at Holden. His hand on hers tightened, and his deep blue eyes searched her face. As if telling her this was it, her last chance to back out of the deal. She licked her lips as his hand warmed hers, and she felt herself nod firmly.

''Good.'' Holden tugged an envelope from an inside pocket and set it on the judge's desk. ''The license,'' he said.

With a sigh, Logan came to stand at Holden's side. Emily hurried to take her spot beside Lucinda. And the judge began to speak. But she barely heard a word he said over the buzzing in her head and the pounding of her heart.

"You may kiss the bride."

Holden took a breath, as nervous as his bride was, he was sure of that. Hell, he knew as well as anyone here that he wasn't good enough for a woman like Lucy Brightwater. But he'd try to be. For a year, he'd try his damnedest not to make her regret this.

He looked down at her. She was still studying the ring he'd placed on her finger, a delicate band of diamonds and amber. Unusual...but then, so was she. It was his search for the perfect ring that had made him late today.

Lucy tipped her head up finally, her eyes wide and dark and full of mystery...secrets. Holden lowered his head and pressed his lips to hers. Soft, and trembling slightly as he kissed them. Parting just a little. Just enough to make his stomach knot and his breath catch in his throat.

When he lifted his head again, her eyes were still closed. Ebony lashes resting on her skin.

"Let me be the first to congratulate you," the judge said, his voice loud, breaking the spell. Lucy's eyes flashed open and Holden managed to shake the man's hand without taking his gaze from hers. Emily Applegate gave her a tentative hug, and then Logan followed suit.

"Welcome to the family, sister," he said gruffly near Lucy's ear. "If my brother gives you any trouble, you let me know, all right?"

Lucy's smile was tremulous, overly bright. "Thanks, Logan."

Logan took Holden's hand then, pumped it hard. "Treat her right, big brother."

Holden nodded. "One more favor, Logan?"

Logan's brows went up. "Why am I not surprised? What is it this time?"

"Don't tell anyone in the family about this just yet."

He heard Lucy's soft gasp and turned toward her. "My God, Holden, you didn't even tell your family you were getting married? Your...mother?"

"No. And I'd prefer they hear it from me. But not today."

Logan shook his head. "News like this is going to leak, Holden. Just how long do you think I can——"

"Just until tomorrow," Holden said. "I just want to give Lucy a day to prepare...before she has to face the lions."

Logan sighed, looking from Holden to Lucy. Then he sent her a smile. "Don't let him shake you. Remember, you *are* one of the lions now."

She said nothing. Still smiling. But it was false, Holden could see that clearly.

"I just have some papers for you to sign and then you can get on with the celebrating," the judge interrupted.

He pushed a sheet at Holden, handed him a pen. Holden signed his name and handed the pen to Lucy. She bent over the desk and scrawled "Lucinda" across the line in an elegant, spiky script. Then she paused with the pen's tip poised on the page. Blinking rapidly, she went on. "Fortune," she wrote.

She sat beside Holden in his hot little car and he drove. They'd spoken of meaningless, trivial things.

Had she packed an overnight bag? Was it all right to leave her cat for the night? Neither of them asking the question foremost in their minds. *Now what?*

"I...would have liked to have taken you on a real honeymoon," Holden said, his tone apologetic.

"I hardly expected that," she replied, frowning at him.

He shook his head. "You deserve that. And a beautiful wedding with all your friends and family there, and a reception going long into the night."

"Do you really think that's what I wanted?"

"Isn't it what every woman wants?"

She shook her head. "I'm not every woman, Holden. And given the circumstances of our marriage, not to mention what's going on in your family right now, I think we did this in the best way possible."

"That's pretty much the rationale I've been using." He licked his lips. "Maybe I can make it up to you...in time."

"There's nothing to make up for." Lucinda leaned her head back against the seat and thoroughly enjoyed having the top down and the wind blowing in her hair. "So where are we going?"

"Someplace special."

"Five-star hotel with all the bells and whistles?" she asked, not looking forward to that prospect at all.

"Sit back and wait. You'll see."

She eyed him, and he sent her a playful wink. Some of the tension between them faded, and she smiled back. "This should be interesting."

"I hope so."

He drove for more than an hour, and Lucinda was

beginning to think he was lost, because for some time now there had been nothing but wild-looking terrain spread out in every direction. It had her worried.

"Holden, do you think we ought to stop and ask for directions?"

He smiled at her again, that charming, knock-'em-dead smile that worked so well on anything with two X chromosomes. "Who would we ask? That prairie dog over there?"

She didn't look at the critter. She'd been seeing them more and more often. "Are we lost?"

"No. As a matter of fact, we're here." As he said it, he turned onto a dirt track that veered off the main road, and brought the car to a stop at a closed gate with a padlock dangling from one side. Jumping out, he pulled a key from his pocket, undid the lock, and swung the big gate wide. Then he got back in and drove through.

Moments later, Lucinda knew she was gaping, but couldn't help herself, because the dirt track curved and she saw, finally, Holden's destination. A two-story log cabin with a double-decker porch on three sides, and a barn-shaped roof, perched along the shore of a lake so still and so clear it looked like a giant mirror reflecting the blue sky. Around it, she could see only trees.

"My God," she whispered. "Holden, this place is incredible." She got out of the car and started forward, so mesmerized she blinked in surprise when he spoke again and she realized he was right beside her.

"Better than a five-star hotel?"

"Better than all of them."

"No heat except the fireplace," he said. "No lights.

We do have a fridge and a water heater that run on LP gas, though, and a generator to run the water pump.''

She didn't care. She didn't care in the least. How could Holden have picked such a perfect place for her? She had never pegged him as the sort of man who would like a cabin in the woods. He seemed so urban, so polished. As excited as a child, she hurried up steps made of logs sawed in two lengthwise, and cupped her hands around her face to peer through the nearest window.

Holden laughed softly, and unlocked the door. "Come on, you'll get a better view from inside."

He held the door for her, and Lucinda walked through, stopping just inside the door, tipping her head back, her gaze moving slowly up the log wall opposite, with its massive cobblestone fireplace and roughly-hewn mantel. Above that an ancient-looking gun rack held two antique weapons, and above them an old photograph, fading black and white, with a few age spots on its face, hung in an oval frame.

"Who is that?" she asked, pointing.

"Kingston Fortune. My grandfather."

The man in the photo didn't look like anyone's grandfather. It had been taken when he was young, late twenties, perhaps. His hair was longish and wavy, probably blond like Holden's. His eyes...were very sexy.

"You look like him," she said.

"You think so?" He sounded surprised, and when she turned it was to see a matching expression on his face.

"You don't think so?"

He shrugged. "I hadn't thought about it. I've been told I look just like my father for so long—"

"Well, your father looked like him, too."

Holden made a sound of derision. "My father was nothing like him. Kingston...he was a hell of a man. You wouldn't believe what he survived in his lifetime."

"No?"

Holden sent her one of his winning smiles. "I'll tell you about him sometime. His tales make great campfire stories."

She lowered her head, averting her eyes. The image that had popped into her mind just then, of the two of them, cozy and warm and intimate in front of the fireplace, rattled her.

That was what she was here for, though. She supposed she'd better get used to the idea.

"Come on, I'll give you the grand tour." He took her arm, leading her by his side through the cabin. The lower level was nearly all one huge room. In this first room, the ceilings towered, cathedral-like, but so rustic. Large beams crossed at the top, and a wagon wheel hung from an ancient-looking black-iron chain in the center. Light fixtures shaped like hurricane lampshades dangled from each spoke of the wheel. Kerosene lamps, all of them. The walls were decked in furs and hides, a bear's head here, a buck with massive antlers over there. The furnishings were clearly chosen for comfort; overstuffed sofa so fat it looked as if a person could get lost in its cushions. Matching love seat and chair. A pair of rockers near the fireplace. A coffee table that was made of no more than a slab sliced off the end of what must have been a giant oak tree, bark still trimming its edges, all of it gleaming beneath thick layers of clear shellac. The floors were hardwood, and woven rugs were scattered here and there for accents.

"This is the living room, and you can see the dining room from here. Basically, it's the same thing." He pointed, she nodded. A large table and chairs held court in the opposite half of this room, their backdrop a row of large windows, and not a curtain in sight. Holden led her over there, and stopped beside those windows.

"Best view on the place," he said.

She nodded in agreement. The windows looked out onto the lake, spreading wide and deep beneath a clear blue sky. Surrounded on all sides, as far as she could tell, by wilderness. Not a smokestack, not a building, not a highway or a telephone pole in sight. "This place is incredible."

"I agree." He nodded toward a doorway with a pair of bat-wing doors its only barrier. "Through there is the kitchen, and there's a pantry and a bathroom off that." Then he led her back across the sprawling living room, past the staircase, to the door on the opposite side. "Through here is a bedroom and another bath. And there are two more bedrooms upstairs."

"It's incredible," she said. "I could be content to stay here forever."

She felt his eyes on her, and looked up to see him staring at her with a look that made her stomach tighten in response. Her cheeks heated, and she lowered her eyes. She was going to sleep with him. Why did that seem to be the only thing she could think about?

"I, um, I'll get our bags," he said.

She nodded. "Good. I'm ready to get out of this dress and into a pair of jeans."

He turned, halfway to the front door, and stared back at her. "You were beautiful today, you know. Prettiest bride I ever saw."

Why was he being so damned *nice* to her? "Thanks, Holden. That's very sweet."

"Wasn't trying to be sweet," he replied, heading once again for the door. "Just honest."

Then he was gone, and she was left to wonder how she was supposed to go through with her not-so-nice little plan when he was trying to make her think he was some kind of saint.

Six

When Holden carried the luggage into the cabin, Lucy was nowhere in sight. But he could hear footsteps, light and quick, coming from above. She must be exploring on her own. He'd thought of bringing her here to give her time to prepare for the moment when she'd have to return with him to face his family—to tell them she was now a Fortune, too. It could be, he realized, a daunting experience. And he didn't want to push it on her until she felt ready.

He didn't want to push anything on her at all. Which was why he intended to honor his agreement to keep his hands to himself. He wasn't going to touch her, or seduce her, or ever mention again that he felt anything beyond friendship for her. Because he didn't want her to start caring back. He didn't want to ruin her life the way his father had ruined his mother's.

He carried the cases upstairs, through the hall, and poked his head around the corner of the open bedroom door. "Find a room you like?"

She'd been standing near the window, gazing out at the lake, but she turned to face him and nodded. "I can see the lake from the bed in this one."

"Then this is the one you get," he said, and set her overnight bag on the foot of the bed. But then he stared at the soft white comforter for a moment. It was rumpled, as if she'd lain upon it for a moment. And he could picture her lying there again...her hair mussed and her eyes sleepy.

"Holden?"

"Hmm?" He didn't look at her, couldn't drag his gaze from the mental image of her in that bed, staring up at him with longing in her eyes. "Damn," he whispered.

Then she was beside him, her hand on his arm. "You okay?"

"What? Oh, um, yeah. Sure."

She frowned at him, a cute little dimple deepening in her cheek. "I was going to ask about the lake. Is it good for swimming?"

"It's the best for swimming," he told her, shaking himself free of the lingering mind warp and focusing on the lady in front of him. "Is that what you'd like to do first? Go swimming?"

Smiling, she nodded. "Seems like the thing to do."

"And then what?" he asked her.

She shrugged. "Play it by ear, I guess."

He nodded. "I'll leave you to change."

She dove from the dock at the water's edge into the crystalline water while Holden sat on the shore, too shaken to do more than watch. He'd been in a sorry state from the moment she'd come down the stairs clad only in her bathing suit. He'd certainly seen gorgeous women in less. In nothing. In bikinis that amounted to little more than nothing. The suit Lucy wore was a demure one-piece tank. No plunging neckline or French-cut leg openings. Just a simple tank. It was red. Spandex. Clingy. Her breasts were round underneath it, her legs, long and shapely and exposed to him, her backside, perfect for squeezing. And he wanted her more than he had before.

Dangerous, this game he was playing. How was he ever going to get through a year without touching her?

She popped out of the water some distance from the dock, and looked back at him. "Aren't you coming in?" she called.

He almost said no. It was too much to ask for him to get into the water with her, to be that close to her. But who was he kidding? He couldn't say no to her. So he got to his feet in his cutoff denim shorts, and walked to the edge of the dock. "How cold is it?" he asked, sticking one foot into the water.

"Freezing! Deliciously freezing."

He made a face. Then he dove into the water, which was even colder than he'd expected. He shivered as he swam, and then emerged right beside her. The droplets that clung to her skin shimmered in the sun, and her hair was slicked back and shiny, making her black eyes seem even larger and darker than before. She slid backward in the water, floating on her back and looking up at the sky. The cold water made her nipples stiff underneath the suit, and he could only stare at them for a long moment.

"Holden?"

"Hmm?"

"Are you going to stand there shivering, or are you going to swim?" She rolled over, and shot off through the water like an errant mermaid, kicking water into his face as she left. Playful. He'd never seen her like this.

Holden shot off after her, catching her easily, and

then they turned and swam back toward the dock together. Holden climbed out, then turned and offered her a hand up. She took it, let him pull her out of the water, then stood beside him with her arms wrapped around her shoulders. He quickly snatched up one of the towels he'd brought down, and draped it over her. His hand slid over her shoulder, lingering there for just a moment before he made himself take it away.

With a sigh, he snatched the other towel and began rubbing himself down with it. And he didn't fail to notice the way she stole glances at him as he did. She seemed to approve of his chest, his abs, which made him glad, and then made him crazy.

Maybe bringing her up here wasn't such a great idea.

"Coming here was a wonderful idea, Holden," she said, and it was so much as if she'd read his mind that he looked up fast. "It's just what we both needed, I think. There's so much tension at home."

He nodded. "How's it going with the baby?"

She blinked, looked up at him. "The...the baby?"

"The preemie?" As he spoke, he turned her and led her back onto the grassy bank. Halfway to the house, a wide wooden bench sat where it had been for the last twenty-odd years, and he took her to it, sat down beside her there.

"Oh, right. It's still touch and go, but she's improving. The mother is home already, but the baby's going to be in the hospital for at least a couple of weeks."

"That's going to be a hell of a bill for someone with no insurance."

Lucy sighed, nodding. "And if they'd had proper

prenatal care, they could have saved themselves all of this." She looked up at Holden. "How about Claudia and Matt? How are they holding up?"

"As well as can be expected, I suppose. Still no sign of Bryan, and not a word from the kidnappers."

"God, your family must be going crazy with worry."

Holden nodded. "That's part of the reason I wanted us to come out here. I didn't want us starting our year together with all that baggage weighing us down."

She looked away. "That was really thoughtful of you."

"Hey, I'm a thoughtful guy."

"Who'd have guessed?"

Holden felt his brows go up. "Was that an insult or a compliment?"

"It was...surprise."

"Hell, I'm full of those. Then again, so's the rest of the family."

"You didn't tell them what we were planning to do today. I'm worried about that."

He eyed her, facing him now, searching him with her dark, probing eyes. "No. I asked Logan to keep it under wraps for now because I'd prefer to tell them myself."

She sighed.

"What?" he asked, instantly worried.

"Nothing. I just...think it might have been better to tell them. It would have given them time to get used to the idea before we get back there."

Holden smiled slowly. "Are you afraid of my family, Lucinda in the Sky?"

Her head came up quickly, eyes going wide. "My God."

"What?"

"You haven't called me that since..." But she didn't finish. She slammed her eyes shut, shook her head.

"I always called you that, Lucy. Just not out loud."

Sighing, she slowly met his eyes again. "Why?"

Holden reached up to gently push a wet tendril of hair off her cheek and tuck it behind her ear. "Because you always seemed...out of reach."

Her brows lifted in surprise. "That's almost funny. If you knew how easily you...that is, how easily you could have..." She closed her eyes and gave her head a shake.

"I knew. But I also knew you deserved better. I'd have only hurt you, Lucy, and I knew myself well enough to know it. I didn't want to do that, so I left you alone."

She blinked slowly. "You mean...you *did* like me? Want me...back then?"

He stared at her for a long moment, seeing a reflection of that adoration that he used to always see in her eyes. "Maybe this isn't such a good subject for us just now." He got to his feet.

To his surprise, Lucy did, as well, gripping his forearm and tugging him around to face her again. "Well, that's too bad, then, because I want to know. My God, Holden, do you know how much your indifference hurt me back then?"

"Indifference?" He closed his eyes, shook his head slowly. "Jeez, Lucy, I was eating my heart out. But it was for your own good."

Mouth agape, she made a sound of disbelief. "It's just like you to think you know what's best for me."

"Oh, come on, Lucy, all of this was over fifteen years ago for crying out loud."

"You admitted you were attracted to me but... Do you still want me, Holden?"

He went utterly still. Searching her face, seeing nothing revealed that she didn't want to reveal, he just stood there, shocked. "What happened to that shy little wallflower I thought I was marrying?"

"She grew up," she said. "Don't tell me you expected me to stay the same lovesick little girl after all this time."

"I...don't know what I expected."

"But not this."

"Lucy, I'm not even sure what *this* is. What do you want from me?"

She shrugged, lowered her head, shaking it. "Nothing."

"Good. Because I don't have anything to give you. Look, Lucy, don't even let yourself begin to think about making more out of what's between us than there is, because I won't. I can't. I thought we were both clear on that."

She narrowed her eyes on him, and the look sent a chill right to his bones. "For my own good?" she asked.

He lied. He lied through his teeth. Because she scared the hell out of him all of the sudden. "Because I'm already itching to get back to my old life-style, Lucy. A different woman every month, sometimes every week. I like it that way."

The blow hit. He saw her flinch, and that meant it

hurt her a little bit. And if it hurt her, that meant she already felt more than she should. Jeez, he hadn't planned on this. He hadn't expected this.

He needed to keep his distance...now more than ever.

Well, he'd certainly made his feelings clear. He might want her...in fact, she was increasingly certain he did. She'd seen his eyes when she'd walked down the stairs in her bathing suit. And when she'd been in the water. And when she got out. He wanted her.

Just like he wanted every halfway-decent-looking female under the age of seventy. He was a womanizer, she reminded herself. Through and through. Always had been. She didn't know why the hell she let herself think for even a moment that he might have changed. Then again, it ought to work in her favor, right?

She put on dry clothes in the bedroom she'd chosen. Jeans and a snug-fitting T-shirt. She was in no mood for seduction tonight. Not after the way he'd slapped her down. Still, time was of the essence here.

But there was something else niggling at her, and she couldn't stop turning it over in her mind, poking at it like a sore tooth. If he wanted her the way he wanted every other woman he met, then why wasn't he trying to have her? Why wasn't he flirting or touching or teasing her? Why?

She didn't understand it, and it was frustrating to think she'd have to work harder than she'd expected to get him to cooperate with her plan. She was not an experienced seductress. She was not an expert lover. She'd never initiated a sexual interlude in her life. She wasn't even certain she could drum up the brass to do it now, when so much depended on it.

Especially with a man who, for some reason only he could know, was unwilling! She'd expected him to go back on his word and start trying to get her into bed the minute they were pronounced man and wife.

Damn him.

She brushed her hair, and then as an afterthought, her teeth, reapplied her deodorant, and finally, she was ready to face him again. She probably wouldn't have the gall to try to initiate anything tonight. Not after he'd made it pretty clear he didn't want her to. But if the opportunity—and the nerve—presented itself, she wanted to be ready. Taking a breath, straightening her spine, she went back downstairs to find her new husband.

Holden had expected this to be easy. She'd seemed like the perfect solution. A woman he respected, liked, even. A woman with no expectations of him, willing to be his wife in name only for a year in exchange for a sizable chunk of change.

Well, thinking it would be that simple had, he supposed, been his first mistake. Nothing was ever easy. But she sure had taken him by surprise. Hell, he still wasn't sure what had happened, but there was a tension brewing between them now, one that hadn't been there before.

He stood at the counter in the kitchen, tossing a salad while a pair of steaks cooked to perfection on the built-in grill. The cabin's pantry was always well stocked, and he'd had the forethought to send someone ahead with fresh produce and perishables, and to turn on the gas-powered fridge to keep it all fresh. After all, it wasn't the first time he'd swept a woman away for a weekend retreat. He had it down to a science.

Not that this time was anything like any of the times before. He'd never been nervous or unsure of himself, never been more confused about what a woman wanted.... Hell, he'd never been married before.

And he'd never been more attentive, every cell in his body attuned and alert, ready to go taut again at the slightest sound from his little wife.

So why was it the sound of her clearing her throat behind him came without any warning whatsoever and made him whirl, dropping salad tongs and a few scraps of lettuce onto the floor?

"Sorry. Didn't mean to startle you."

She was laughing at him behind that innocent expression. He could tell. "Uh, I didn't hear you come in, is all." Glancing down at the mess on the floor, he noted that she was in her sock feet. No wonder she'd sneaked up on him so silently. Then as he hunkered down to gather up the salad tongs, his gaze moved up her legs, over faded blue jeans that hugged her hips and crawled between her thighs the way he wanted to do.

Oh, hell. Above that was a snug white T-shirt. Not a loose-fitting one like he might wear himself, but a tiny one that hugged her so close he could see a strip of tanned midriff between it and her jeans. And he could also see that she was braless underneath it. Her gleaming black hair brushed the shoulders of that white shirt in stark contrast, and the white she wore made her dark eyes even darker.

She was one incredible hunk of woman.

"Holden?"

"Hmm?" He lifted his head, to look up into her eyes.

"You, um, waiting to be knighted or something?"

He was practically kneeling at her feet. And knighthood was the last thing on his mind. Knights were honorable and noble and all of that. Hell, he'd have been drummed right out of his armor for the sultry thoughts in his head. He got to his feet, avoiding her eyes so she wouldn't see the raw hunger in his, and turned to the sink to wash the tongs.

"Steak smells good," she said, moving toward the grill and picking up a fork to poke the thick cuts of meat as they sizzled.

"Hope you're hungry," he rasped. He was back at his salad bowl, adding chopped tomatoes and tossing it again.

"Starved," she said. "And I think my steak is done enough. I like 'em rare." She reached for one of the plates he had sitting out at the same time he did, and they collided, chest to chest. Holden looked down at her. She let his eyes probe hers, and left her body right where it was, pressed up tight. Her breasts mashed against his chest, her face only a couple of inches away.

She was supposed to pull back. She was supposed to be embarrassed. Okay, maybe she was embarrassed, if the color staining her cheeks was anything to go by. But she was *not* pulling away.

Holden finally managed to do that himself. "Um...sorry."

"Don't be silly, Holden. You didn't hurt me. And we are married."

"Yeah, but..."

She sent him a sidelong glance, even while stabbing her steak and dropping it onto her plate. "But what?"

"Nothing."

Shrugging, she set her plate aside. "Want me to get yours off?" she asked, reaching for the second plate, a question in her eyes.

"Uh, no. I like mine cooked." He glanced at her steak. "At least enough so they don't moo when I stick the fork in them."

"You'll cook all the flavor out."

"I just don't happen to like biting down on things that wiggle."

She lifted her brows. "That's not the way I heard it."

Holden almost gaped. But he managed to hide his surprise and return his attention to the salad. His throat was dry, though, and the skin on the back of his neck tingling. His belly was tight, his temperature, he thought, heading upward.

If he ever got through this night it would be a miracle.

"So, um, what kind of dressing do you want on your salad?" he asked. Safe subject. Salad dressing.

Her reply was to turn to the refrigerator and open it, scanning the bottles inside. "Oh, hey. This looks good."

He turned, expecting to see her holding a bottle of Italian or Ranch. Instead, she was lifting a bottle of wine. Her hand curled around its slender neck while the fingers of the other one slid down over the label. He'd told the local grocer he always ordered from to stock the place with the usual things. Forgetting that the usual things included wine. Because any self-respecting womanizer would always have some on hand to help things along. Only in this case, he didn't want to help things along.

But she was already rummaging in a cupboard for wineglasses, setting a pair of them on the counter, pulling open a drawer in search of a corkscrew. Holden took the bottle from her. "Here, I'll get it."

She found the corkscrew and put it into his hand. Holden opened the wine, and had to move closer to her to pour it. When he stopped with the glass half full, she put her hand over his on the bottle, and pressed downward until he filled it the rest of the way. She did the same when he filled the second glass. He met her eyes. "Trying to get me drunk, Lucy?"

She looked away. "I think it would take more than that to get you drunk, Holden. You forget, I've seen you drink before."

"As I recall, you didn't like it much."

She lifted her brows, and her glass, taking a deep sip while his gaze riveted itself to her lips. "Now, what makes you say that?"

"You pretty much ignored me after that night at the Valentine's Day dance," he said. Then he shook his head. "I've always assumed I must have acted like an idiot when you drove me home that night."

"No," she said. "Actually, that was the next day."

"What was?"

"Nothing. Never mind. Get your steak, Holden, before it burns."

He set the bottle down, rescued the steak, and dropped it onto the remaining plate. And before he turned back around, Lucy was heading out of the kitchen, through those bat-wing doors and into the dining area with her plate, her glass, and the rest of the bottle tucked under one arm. Holden sighed, watching her go. The view from behind made him take a deep drink of wine from his glass and square his shoulders, before he gathered up his own plate and went in there to join her.

Seven

She'd never been more nervous in her life. So she drank a bit too much wine with dinner, and by the time they finished eating, she no longer had any idea how much of the wine Holden had ingested, and how much she had. She only knew the bottle was empty, and her lips were tingly. She'd intended to keep track of how much he drank. Maybe it would mellow him out a little.

Hell, it had worked last time.

Holden got up and started gathering up the empty dishes. She got up too, and covered his hand with hers. "Let me get those."

He shook his head. "Why? 'Cause you're the female?"

"No. Because I would rather you be doing something else just now." She saw the wariness come into his eyes.

"What?" His voice was slightly hoarse.

"Building a fire."

He glanced in toward the fireplace, then back at her. "It's June, Lucy."

"Yes, but it's not too hot here. And I really would like a fire."

Sighing, he lifted his hands in surrender. "Okay. I'll build a fire."

He headed into the front room. Lucinda quickly cleared their plates from the table, carried them into the kitchen, and washed them up. It took all of five minutes. While she was out there, she located another bottle of wine. But she was already feeling pretty unsteady on her feet; she wasn't used to drinking much. Maybe she'd better not have any more. She needed to keep her head tonight. She'd hate like hell to wake up in the morning and not remember whether he'd capitulated or not. Still, it wouldn't hurt to get a bit more down him.

When she went back into the living room, with freshly filled glasses, vowing that she wasn't going to touch hers, Holden was already adding larger logs to the fire. She paused by the big kerosene lamp on the end table, and bent to blow it out.

Holden spun around. "What did you do that for?"

"The fire is plenty of light. Besides, it has to be dark to get the full effect."

"I've used that line a time or two myself," he muttered.

"What?"

"Nothing."

Shrugging, she went forward, set the glasses on the tree slab coffee table, and sank onto the incredibly soft sofa.

Holden stood between her and the fire for a long moment. "I'm, uh...pretty tired," he began.

"Oh, come on, Holden. Sit with me. Tell me some of those family stories about Kingston up there. I'm dying to hear them. And you did say they made perfect fireside tales."

"I did say that, didn't I?"

"Yes, you did."

With a sigh, he came to the sofa and lowered himself onto it. "All right. If a bedtime story is what you want, I'll play."

If he'd play, she thought, she wouldn't need to ask for a bedtime story. But at least it would keep him here longer at her side. And there might be a chance...

"My great-grandmother didn't give birth to Kingston. She found him on the doorstep of her home in Iowa, and even though she and her husband had children of their own, and few resources, they decided to keep him and raise him as one of the family. He had a birthmark on his lower back, a three-pronged crown. So they named him Kingston, called him King for short."

She leaned back on the sofa, finding herself interested in the tale, even though she'd only asked to hear it as a ploy to keep him close. "Did they ever find out where he really came from?"

"No. They never did. I wonder sometimes, though. It's odd, not knowing."

Turning toward him, pulling her legs beneath her, Lucinda studied his face, and Kingston's. "You... you're clearly Anglo-Saxon." Moving her hands, she ran one finger over the bridge of his nose. "You have King's nose. Strong. And his chin," she touched it as she spoke. "I'll bet there's some Scot in your blood."

"You think so?"

"Mmm. Yes. I do." Holden closed his hand around hers and moved it gently away from his face. Sighing in defeat, Lucinda settled down beside him, much closer than before. So close, her side was touching his, and though she leaned her head back against the cushion, she could easily tilt it to the side and rest it on his shoulder if she wanted to. He wasn't moving away from her, and that was encouraging. "Tell me more."

"I think you've had too much wine," he said.

"I don't remember there being anything in our agreement about not drinking wine."

"There wasn't."

"I didn't think so. Tell me more about your grandfather."

He drew a deep breath, sighed. "He worked for a local farmer when he was a young man, fell in love with the man's daughter. But the old farmer was a bible-thumping sort who didn't think King was good enough. So the two ran away to St. Louis and got married, never telling him where they'd gone. For a little while they were happy. Had a baby boy named Teddy. He's one of the many family mysteries. No one knows whatever became of poor Teddy Fortune."

"Why not?"

Holden looked down at her, and he seemed more relaxed now that he was involved with the retelling of the family history. She leaned her head on his shoulder and sighed with satisfaction when his arm came around hers.

"World War Two happened. It was around forty-two, when King had to go and serve. While he was away, his wife got sick and died. Someone contacted her father, and the old bastard showed up to take Teddy away. That was the last anyone ever heard of him."

"But...Teddy would be your uncle. Surely Kingston searched for him when he returned?"

"It was two years before he could make his way home. His ship went down, he was wounded, spent several days stranded on an island with a comrade. King saved a lot of lives when the ship went down, collected a few medals. But this buddy of his saved his life on that island. In the end, King made it back, and Judd didn't. But before he died, Judd Hobbs gave King a locket with a lock of golden-blond hair inside, and asked King to make sure he was buried with it.

"When King got back, his first priority was trying to find his son, Teddy. When every attempt failed, time and time again, he moved on with his life. Decided to pay Hobbs's widow a visit, out of respect for his fallen comrade. He'd been given a hefty compensation check for his injury…it was his leg, as I recall. So he figured he ought to make sure the widow of the man who saved his life was being taken care of. He also thought he'd give the locket to her, since he had no idea where Hobbs was buried. He thought it would mean something to her to know how much her husband thought of her."

"Honorable. Is that how he wound up in Texas?"

"That's how he wound up in Texas. Hobbs's widow was my grandmother, Selena."

"Selena," she repeated. "Mexican?"

"Half. Granddad found her living on the ranch left to her by her father, running it single-handedly as best she could. So King stayed on to help."

"And gave her the locket?"

"Not exactly. See, when he met Selena, he was pretty surprised to see that she had very dark hair. Nowhere near blond like what was in the locket."

Lifting her head and her brows at once, Lucy said, "Uh-oh."

"Yeah, uh-oh. Turns out Hobbs only married Selena to get his hands on her ranch. He was actually in love with her sister."

"The blonde?"

"Right. Anyway, Hobbs had a brother still living, Malcolm. And Malcolm had it in his head that he wanted that ranch. Eventually, he tried to murder my grandmother to get it, but King got the best of him, and in the end, he married Selena, and the two of them built the ranch into what it is today."

"And had two sons. Your father, Cameron, and your uncle Ryan."

"And a daughter, my aunt Miranda."

Lucinda frowned, tilting her head to one side, but the room tilted slightly with it. "I've never met her, have I?"

"No. She ran off...I think it was the year Logan was born. I was about five or so. They say she headed for Hollywood, with her heart set on becoming a big star. But she didn't leave on very good terms with the family, and I don't think anyone's heard from her since. Gosh, she was only seventeen when she left. She'd be forty-six now."

"You remember her?"

Holden nodded. "Yeah. I loved her. She was a teenage rebel, outspoken, disagreed with her parents over everything. And gorgeous, too. A real blond bombshell. She always said she'd be as big as Marilyn was someday. But I guess we'd have heard about it if she'd made it." He sighed. "I wonder what happened to her."

"Maybe someday you'll find out."

"I hope so." He gazed into the fire for a long moment. Lucinda followed that gaze, watched the flames dancing, smelled the resin burning.

"This is nice," she said.

"Yeah, well, it's getting late."

She sighed, but didn't get up. She only tipped her face up to his, knowing her moment was slipping away, and wondering why she wasn't as disappointed as she'd expected to be. She'd enjoyed spending this time with him. Just...talking.

"So, do I know all the family secrets now?"

"What're you, kidding? We have volumes."

She smiled. "Gives me something to look forward to, then."

"Yeah?"

"Mm-hmm. You tell a hell of a bedtime story, you know."

He smiled at her, seeming to get lost in her eyes for a long moment. But then he finally dragged his gaze away and got to his feet. "I'm going to turn in."

Lucinda closed her eyes, lowered her head. "Are you...sure you want to?"

He was quiet for a moment. Then he asked, very softly, "Just what do you mean by that, Lucy?"

Biting her lip, still not facing him, she forced the words to come. "It's our wedding night, Holden. And while you gave me your word you'd be faithful, I've been thinking that maybe...a year of celibacy is a bit much to ask."

His hand came to cup her chin, and he gently tipped her face up so he could search it. She felt heat, embarrassment, fear he'd take her up on her offer, and fear he'd throw it back in her face. "Are you offering, Lucy?"

She nodded in a quick, jerky motion.

Holden licked his lips, closed his eyes. She got to her feet, putting her hands on his shoulders to steady herself. And the next thing she knew she was wrapped tight in his arms and he was kissing her hard. She twined her arms around his neck, parted her lips for him, let him in. Even moved her hips, rubbing against him in a way that should let him know she meant what she said.

Eventually, Holden lifted his mouth from hers. "You taste...like wine," he whispered. Then, biting his lip, he let go of her so suddenly she fell down onto the sofa. "Damn, Lucy, you're drunk. You don't know what the hell you're doing."

"How do you know that?" she asked him. "How do you know I'm not perfectly aware of what I'm doing?"

"Because if you did, you wouldn't be doing it."

"Don't be so sure about that, Holden."

He spun away, pushing a hand through his hair. "Lucy, listen to me. I don't want this. I don't want to risk you starting to feel anything for me. I don't want you to want me, Lucy."

"I do, though. I...always have," she whispered.

"Then this was a mistake. Dammit, you can't let yourself, because I'll only hurt you in the end."

"You already hurt me," she said as she stood. "I survived it once, I can handle it again. I'm a big girl now. Hell, I was only seventeen then, and I got through it okay."

Holden went very still, his back to her. Slowly, he

turned, clasping her shoulders, scanning her face and making her shamefully aware of what she'd just revealed to him, and of the hot tears sliding slowly over her cheeks.

"You don't want me," she whispered. "You didn't want me then, either. It was just the booze, wasn't it, Holden? It never meant a damn thing to you, did it?"

His eyes intense, he stared hard into hers. "Lucy, what are you talking about?"

She drew a breath. "I'm talking about the night you slept with me. The night I had sex for the first time, Holden. I'm talking about you passing out on top of me, and how ashamed I felt...and how hopeful. It didn't matter to me how wrong it was...it was all okay with me, because I thought it meant something. But it didn't, did it, Holden?"

"My God," he whispered. "Dammit, Lucy, I didn't—"

"Oh, yes, you did. And you didn't even remember it the next day. So the way I see it, Holden, you owe me. And it's my turn to collect. But all of a sudden, you've developed some kind of aversion to casual sex with a woman who means nothing to you. When the hell did that happen, huh? When, I'd like to know?"

"Lucy, stop. Wait. Lucy..."

She pressed her hands to her forehead. "God, you were right. I've had too much wine." She turned and walked fast toward the door. "I'm going for a walk."

"You're not going anywhere." He gripped her arm from behind. "I want to talk about this."

"Well, I don't. I said way too much, Holden. Just let me get the hell out of your sight for a while so I can try to salvage some scrap of my pride here. Please..."

He held up both hands. Lucy wrenched the door open and stalked outside into the darkness.

Holden let her go. The night air might do her some good, he supposed. Certainly couldn't make matters any worse. So he'd just give her some time. Give himself some time.

My God, what the hell had happened to his simple plan? This was supposed to be a friendly business arrangement. And he already knew where he'd gone wrong. He'd let himself believe in her facade. The mask she'd been wearing—the one that said she had no feelings whatsoever for him. The one that lied. She felt something. Anger, at him for having forgotten that night. Pain at what she perceived as his rejection of her back then.

He closed his eyes, remembering. He'd seen her the next day. And he'd been with that giggling blonde, whatever the hell her name was. He remembered Lucy's surprised look and the way she'd averted her eyes, spoken quickly and softly, and hurried away. She must have been expecting... God, she must have been expecting so much.

Lowering his head, Holden pressed the bridge of his nose between his fingers. "Well, you were right, Dad. I turned out just like you. The same kind of selfish, callous son of a gun. Poison to a decent woman."

He'd been so determined not to ruin Lucy's life, not to cause her the kind of pain his father had caused his mother. But it looked as though he'd already done all of that, a long time ago. Took her virginity and then forgot about it.

And the worst part was, the poor thing thought she still wanted him. Or maybe that was just the wine. Either way, he'd rejected her again tonight, hurt her again tonight. And he hadn't meant to do that.

He glanced up toward the door. Okay, she'd been alone long enough. She shouldn't be wandering around outside in the dark in her condition anyway. He didn't know what the hell he was going to say when he caught up to her, but he guessed he'd better think of something fast.

The wind had picked up outside. And it was dark, the sky thick with a blanket of clouds that blotted out the stars, the moon. No light danced on the water tonight. He supposed it was fitting.

Lucy sat on the dock. He could just make out the shape of her there, on the edge, her feet hanging over, dangling in the water maybe. When he got closer, he saw her socks balled up beside her. Her jeans were rolled up.

"I didn't come out here so you'd have to come chasing after me," she said, not turning around. The wind whispered harder, its breath riffling her hair.

"I'm sorry, Lucy." It was the only thing he could think of to say.

"So am I."

"You don't have anything to be sorry for." He moved forward, heeled off his shoes, and sat down beside her.

"Yes, I do. I shouldn't have lashed out at you like that for something that happened so long ago." She looked sideways at him, and he thought she'd been crying, but it was hard to be sure in the darkness. "I didn't plan to ever tell you. But I guess I've been holding it in for so long it just…had to come out."

"I wish you had told me then."

"What good would that have done?"

Holden shrugged. "Hell, I don't know." A deep sigh worked out of him, and he knew what he had to do. "Look, I'll let you out of our bargain. We don't have to go on with this—"

"No." She said it quickly, her voice louder than before. Then, more softly, "No, Holden. I intend to stick to the deal we made."

Slowly he shook his head. "But this *isn't* the deal we made. Lucy, I wanted a business arrangement. No emotions involved. This is—this was—a mistake."

She looked at him for a long time, though he doubted she could see him very clearly. "What are you so afraid of, Holden? It's not as if I can force you to start to have feelings for me. No one's going to make you care."

"It's not me I'm worried about." He said it too quickly, without thinking first. Saw her flinch. "That didn't come out right."

"No, I think it came out just right. There's no way in hell you will ever feel a thing for me, so that's not your concern."

"Lucy—"

"What is, then? Are you afraid I'll start to care about you? Use some kind of guilt trip to make you stay with me beyond the limits of our agreement?"

"You wouldn't do that."

"No," she said softly. "I wouldn't."

He swallowed hard, and his throat was bone dry.

He felt as if he were walking blind through a mine-field. "I just don't want to end up hurting you, Lucy. That's all. I've watched my mother all my life, loving a man who was incapable of loving her back the way she deserved to be loved. And I made a vow a long time ago that I'd never put any woman through that."

She turned her head and stared out at the black water. The wind blew stronger now, and her hair flew around her. "You're awfully full of yourself, Holden Fortune. Let me just reassure you, I am not in love with you. I am not going to fall in love with you. I'm sorry you got the wrong impression in there, but the only thing I was suggesting was..." She didn't finish.

"Sex," he said. "And you can't even say it. Because you're not the kind of woman who would have casual, meaningless sex, Lucy, and we both know it."

"You don't know anything about me at all," she said. "Yes, I wanted sex. I'm a grown woman, and there's nothing wrong with that. Nice girls have needs, too, you know. They feel desire. I'm not a porcelain doll, Holden, and I'm not frigid. Just because I'm not one of your bimbos of the month, doesn't mean I'm not a real woman."

"I know that."

She nodded, still not looking him in the eye. "I am not willing to go without having sex for a year. And you're not capable of it. We can engage in extramarital affairs and cause yet another Fortune family scandal...or we can do the sensible thing and sleep together."

"That all sounds very clinical and logical to you, I'll bet," he said slowly. Inside he was burning. With the desire to take her up on her offer and show her just how explosive it would be between them—and with a newborn fury at her suggestion that she would look elsewhere for sexual satisfaction. "I'll tell you what, Doc. We are not going to engage in any extra-marital affairs. If I can stay faithful, then you can sure as hell do the same. And if it gets to be too frustrating, I suggest a little manual labor."

She sucked in a sharp little gasp, looking up quickly.

"Oh, yeah, I can see how open-minded you are about sex. You're shocked by the very suggestion, aren't you?"

She said nothing, just glared at him.

"That's the deal. If you can't live with it, then we'll get this thing annulled tomorrow morning. If you can, then you'll get your money. But keep it clear in your mind, Lucy, I'm paying for a business arrangement, not for sex."

"You're a bastard, Holden."

"That's right. That's the point. Now that I've re-minded you of it, this ought to be a little easier." He got to his feet. The wind whipped at his shirt, and he thought he heard thunder rumble in the distance. "Come on inside now. It's going to storm."

"I'll come inside when I'm damned good and ready."

"You'll come inside now. You're drunk, it's dark, and you're sitting on the edge of a lake with a hun-dred-foot drop-off." And besides that, he thought, he couldn't pull off this act much longer. He wanted her. He cared for her, and he damn well didn't want to admit to either of those things.

"I want to stay out here."

"Damn." He bent down, put his hands underneath her arms, and pulled her to her feet. She didn't fight, didn't pull away. Just went stiff and looked murderous. "Please come inside," he said.

Lightning flashed and he saw her tears. Realized that must be why she didn't want to come in, she didn't want him to see that she'd been crying. "Lucy—"

Another flash, an earsplitting crack, and then a roar as a tree crashed to the ground a few yards away. Lucy jumped in surprise, losing her balance, and even as Holden saw what was happening, he couldn't stop it. The sky split open, rain pummeled the earth, and Lucy splashed into the cold, black water.

Her arms, his shoulders bare around him and she was wet.

Smith opened her eyes softly. "All right, it's okay." His arms came back around her, inside his shirt this time, so warm, soothing, and she moved against them, so warm.

Eight

The water seemed to close in around her, and it was so unexpected that she swallowed some, choked, and swallowed some more, as she flailed her arms and kicked her legs, striving for the surface.

Then Holden was there. She felt his strong arms around her, pulling her upward. She broke surface, gasping, choking, water running over her face, her hair in her eyes. But his hands pushed it away, palms smooth on her wet skin.

"Are you okay?" He shouted the question, making her aware of the now roaring wind, the pounding rain, the crashing thunder growing louder all the time. Blinking her eyes open, she was immediately blinded by strobelike flashes of lightning, and Holden's face seemed to flicker before her.

Then he was pulling her, and she could only assume they were heading toward the dock. No, that was wrong, the shore itself. No sooner did her feet touch the bottom in the shallower waters than she felt herself lifted off them. And Holden carried her the rest of the way, up out of the water, sloshing through it to the shore beyond. Once on dry land, he ran, still carrying her. Only seconds seemed to pass before he was kicking the door closed behind him, and carrying her to the sofa, lowering her onto it. He pulled his arms from beneath her, but she closed hers around him and clung, shivering.

"All right," he said softly. "All right, it's okay." His arms came back around her, and he held her close for a long moment. "You're okay, now, all right? Hmm?"

Nodding hard against his shoulder, she said, "I'm f-freezing."

"I know. Hold on, okay?"

Again she nodded, and this time when he pulled away, she let him go. She hugged herself, shaking, watching Holden in the firelight. He didn't walk. He ran, first to the fireplace to jam several more chunks of wood into the flames, then up the stairs. She couldn't stop shivering. The fire's warmth barely seemed to be touching her here. Getting off the sofa, she moved closer to the fireplace, and sank to the floor right in front of it, her knees drawn to her chest, her arms wrapped around them.

Only moments later Holden was back again, his arms loaded down. He set the stack of towels and things down on the floor, and knelt beside her. "Loosen up your arms for me," he said, and when she did, he peeled her dripping wet T-shirt off over her head.

Wearing no bra, she automatically crossed her arms in front of her chest. But Holden only paused for a second, his gaze lingering on her breasts for an instant before he jerked it away as if by force, and reached for a towel. Gently, he rubbed her down. Her back, her arms. Her shoulders and neck. Her belly. Then he draped the towel around her, and snatched up another to rub at her wet hair. When he finished, he said, "Stand up, let's get you out of those jeans."

Still shaking with cold, she let him help her to her feet, and stood there, amazed and mesmerized as he undid her jeans and shoved the wet denim down over her hips, panties and all. As he pushed the jeans down, he bent, as well, and when he knelt at her feet, his eyes were on her body. His gaze sliding up and down her, until he closed his eyes tight.

"Hold on to my shoulders and pull your feet out," he instructed in a voice that seemed too choked to speak above a harsh whisper.

She braced her hands on Holden's shoulders and pulled first one foot, then the other, free of the wet, clinging denim. He reached for another towel, his eyes open again, and so attentive that she almost burned with embarrassment. There was no part of her that was hidden to those eyes as he began running the towel up and down her legs. Her thighs.

She wasn't shivering anymore. His hands went still, and Lucy looked down at him, saw the raw hunger dancing with the firelight in his eyes.

"Holden..."

"Here." He pressed the towel into her hand and got to his feet. Still, his gaze roamed her flesh until he forcibly turned his back to her. He picked up a plush terry robe from the stack of things he'd carried down. "Put this on. Wrap up in a blanket, and sit by the fire until you're warm."

She took the robe from him. "Thank you."

"*De nada,*" he muttered. "I'm, uh, gonna go get changed myself."

"All right."

He waited a moment, a long, tense moment, that made her wonder if he were battling the urge to turn around again and strip the towel off her. She wasn't sure if she hoped he would or feared he would. But then he snatched up the remaining pile of towels, and the second robe she saw resting atop them, and headed into the nearest bathroom.

Holden closed the bathroom door behind him, and stood in the darkness, jaw tight, fists clenched at his sides. He was dripping wet, freezing cold, and burning up inside all at once, and the physical chaos of all of it was only a dim reflection of what was going on in his mind.

"St. Francis of Assisi couldn't have survived this kind of temptation," he muttered to himself in the darkness. And immediately, he felt like a fool. So he desired her. So what? He'd desired a great number of women. He'd had most of them.

That was all this was, then, he decided. He wanted her, and he'd decided he couldn't have her, and that was the reason the wanting seemed to be growing larger by the second. That was the reason that it was taking over his mind and his soul and his body. That was the only reason. He'd deemed her forbidden fruit, and that made her seem twice as sweet.

God, she seemed sweet. When he stripped her clothes away…when he knelt in front of her and just looked his fill…. Her skin, bronze and satin-smooth, gleaming with water and firelight. Her breasts, round and high. Proud, dark centers and small rigid nipples. Her belly, so flat and tight, and the darkness of her navel like a shadow of sin, calling to him. The curls between her legs were raven, gleaming, soft. Her thighs were—

"Enough!"

Holden braced his hands against the wall, let his head hang down between his arms. "Enough," he whispered. "Just stop thinking about her. Just stop."

Impossible. Man, his father must be having a hell of a laugh at him now. A hell of a laugh. The old bastard…it was as if he'd been determined to make sure Holden was destined to turn out just like him. Oh, yeah, the rest of the family thought this final act of Cameron's—the changing of his will—had been to protect Holden from becoming like his father. But in fact, it had only forced him to do just that. He'd married a good woman. And dammit, he was going to ruin her life.

No. No, he wouldn't. He would not make Lucy's life the hell his mother's had been. He refused.

And that was that.

Slowly, he stood straight again, and began peeling off his freezing, wet clothes. He took his time changing. A long, hot shower to chase the chill out of his bones would have been nice. He might have wished for a cold one, but if that dip in the frigid lake hadn't helped dampen his desire for his *wife* then a cold shower wasn't going to help, either. Anyway, it didn't matter because he didn't dare leave her alone for that long. So he settled for toweling himself dry, and donning the warm robe he'd brought with him, all in utter darkness, because he hadn't bothered to bring a lamp in here. Didn't matter, he told himself. He may be losing his mind, but he still knew where everything was.

Lucy had misunderstood everything he'd said to her, before all hell broke loose outside. She thought he didn't want her, but he did. She thought he was so immune to her that there was no risk whatsoever of his coming to care anything about her. But he already cared. That was why he was so determined not to let her do the same. Not to hurt her. And he'd only blown up at her the way he had in some stupid, primitive, knee-jerk reaction to her threat—and yes, it had been precisely that—that she would find what she needed elsewhere.

Still, maybe it was best she'd interpreted his clumsy words the way she had. Let her think him cold and callous, utterly incapable of feeling anything real for anyone except himself. Let her believe it. Because as long as she did, she'd be safe. Her heart would be safe. And she wouldn't let him break it.

That thought firm in his mind, he ventured back into the main room. The rain still pounded on the roof, smacked against the windowpanes. Thunder still sounded like some overzealous drummer in a heavy metal band. Lightning still flickered, turning the entire cabin into a faulty neon sign.

Lucy was curled up on her side, sleeping near the fireplace. A heavy blanket wrapped tight around her, her knees drawn up, head pillowed by her hands. The firelight danced over her, and the lightning, when it flashed, made her glow like an angel. His temptation, right?

Holden wandered to the door, checked the lock, glanced outside, but couldn't make a good guess at the damage in the flickering light. It would have to wait until morning. He turned back again, walked slowly over to where Lucy lay on the floor. He didn't suppose he ought to leave her there all night. He should scoop her up, carry her up the stairs, and tuck her into her bed.

Or maybe he could just smash his head against the cobblestone hearth a few times. Either one would be equally painful.

With a sigh, he bent and gathered her into his arms, his hands skimming across warm flesh. As soon as he straightened, her face turned toward the crook of his neck. Her lips nuzzled him there, and her arms linked around him. The faster he got her tucked in and got away from her, the better, he decided, and he turned to start toward the stairs. But when he did, the blanket fell away. And there was nothing else. She hadn't donned the robe as he'd told her to. She'd just burrowed under the covers and fallen asleep.

And now she was naked in his arms. Firelight painted her skin. The thunder rumbled and at first he thought the sound had come from within him. Her head came up off his shoulder and she looked up into his eyes; hers dark and gleaming in the fireglow. Flashing with the lightning. Then she pressed her mouth to his, and this time the rumble did come from him. A deep groan of anguished need that he couldn't contain.

He kissed her. He kissed her mouth, and when it parted, he went inside, pushing his tongue between her lips and rubbing hers with it. She tasted good. Warm, sweet, eager. He slid his mouth along her jaw, tasting her skin, and then her throat, her neck, flicking his tongue as he went. She made a soft sound, part sigh, part moan. He lifted her higher in his arms so that her back arched toward him and her head fell backward. Her breasts were presented to him, an offering he could not refuse. He bent his head to them, and then he held her to him as he caught a nipple in his mouth and began to suck at it. Lucy's hands dove into his hair, and she pulled his head closer, harder against her, straining to press herself into his hungry mouth.

"Please, Holden..." she whispered.

He closed his teeth lightly on her nipple, and when she responded with a shivering whimper, he bit harder, tugging, pinching it between his teeth, and then releasing her again to lick and nurse the sting away. He pulled his arm from beneath her legs, lowering her feet to the floor, his mouth still clamped to her breast, his body bending over hers.

Her hands pushed the robe from his shoulders, then ran over his flesh, kneading him, rubbing him, holding herself to him. And he was naked, and hard, and wanting her. He lifted his head from her breast, and straightening, stared hard into her eyes. "I hope you're sure this is what you want."

Her answer was to tighten her arms around his neck and slowly lift her legs until they were wrapped around his middle. "It's what we both want," she whispered, rubbing herself against him.

Holden's hands slid lower, cupped her buttocks, lifted her a little, until her position was just right. And then slowly, he slid himself inside her. His eyes slammed closed, and his body went rigid with the feel of her wrapped so tight around him. She clung to him harder as he went deeper, harder still when he drew back. Holden found her mouth once again, and fed from it as he moved her body up and down upon his.

He felt her muscles clenching in anticipation, tightening more and more as he drove harder, deeper, pushing her limits, taking her closer. He watched her face in between kisses. Saw the passion on it as the lightning flashed and the fire leaped. And just as she cried out his name in a hoarse, tortured voice, he, too, reached his climax and spilled himself into her as his head spun and his body sang.

Spent, he fell to his knees, with Lucy still twined around him. She didn't seem to want to let go. Her face was buried on his chest, and he thought he felt dampness there. God, was she crying?

"Lucy?"

A shuddery sigh. She eased up her grip, pulled away slightly, and looked up into his eyes. "I...didn't realize it was...supposed to be..."

Holden lifted a hand, fingered a strand of her hair. "I shouldn't have—"

"It's all right." She lowered her chin, lifted it again. "So long as you don't forget about it by morning."

"I won't forget about it in a hundred years."

She offered a shaky smile. "You see, now, don't you? You were worrying for nothing. We had sex. I feel much better now." She averted her eyes. "And I didn't do anything foolish like falling head over heels in love with you in the process."

Holden watched as she eased away, pulling her fallen blanket with her, and curling once more into her little nest on the floor near the fire, her back to him.

And he thought he heard a little voice in his head whispering, *That makes one of us.*

Yeah, right. That had to be the most ridiculous thought he'd ever had.

* * *

Lucy woke up on the sofa, not on the floor where she'd gone to sleep, and she figured she had Holden to thank for that. He probably hadn't dared risk carrying her up to her own bed. She might have stirred awake and made him—

Lucy closed her eyes and groaned as she remembered what she'd done last night. Good Lord, where had all of that come from? The venomous way she'd spilled her guts about what had happened between them that night back in high school. The emotional reaction when he'd made it clear that he felt nothing for her now. The seduction later on. The…enthusiasm with which she'd made love to him.

It wasn't her. None of that was her. Or it didn't used to be. Now…Lord, now everything seemed different. *She* seemed different. Like a stranger to herself.

"Good morning." His voice was low, wary, and coming from the other end of the room.

She turned her head toward it, even though she'd have rather buried it in her pillows.

"You still speaking to me?" he asked.

Squeezing her eyes tight, she nodded. "I should probably be the one asking you that question."

"No, you're wrong there." He sighed, and she opened her eyes to face him once more. "How are you feeling this morning?"

Lucy shrugged while doing a quick self-analysis. "Slight headache. Not bad, though. And a bad case of cotton-mouth."

"A cup of coffee will fix that right up," he said, and he ducked through the bat-wing doors, and emerged a second later with a filled cup. "Cream and one sugar, right?'' Crossing the room, he set the cup on the big coffee table.

"How'd you know?'' God, it smelled heavenly. And there were other scents wafting her way now. Bacon. She could hear it sizzling, too.

"I've seen you drink coffee a couple of times before. At the Double Crown, and the hospital cafeteria.''

And remembered, she thought. Very odd thing for a man like him to do. She lifted the steaming cup to her lips, took a sip, and set it down again in its saucer. "You make good coffee.''

"Yeah, well, it's a start.''

Lucy looked at him. He seemed nervous, not at all his usual confident ladies' man self. "Holden...''

"Lucy...'' he said at the same time.

She managed a smile, though it was awkward. "You first,'' she said.

"Okay. I owe you an apology. Several apologies, in fact. I really don't think there's any way I can make all of this up to you. But I'm going to try.''

She blinked. This was not what she had expected to hear from him this morning. "For what?'' she finally asked.

"Oh, come on. For everything. I took advantage of your crush on me when you were an innocent teenager. I took advantage of your condition last night when you had too much wine. I hurt you both times with my cavalier attitude, and I—I'm just sorry, Lucy. More sorry than I can say.''

Licking her lips, lowering her gaze, she said, "As I recall, Holden, I'm the one who initiated...things. Both times.''

"But I knew better. And it doesn't matter. Look, Lucy, if you've changed your mind and want out of this arrangement, just say the word."

He looked at her, waiting. She drew a breath. "Do you want out of it?"

His brows drew together. "I don't know how to answer that."

"Well, neither do I."

He nodded, maybe seeing the futility of asking such a question now that it had been turned around on him. "If we stick with it...then I'd like for us to start over."

"Start over?"

"Clarify the terms of our arrangement, and start over. No misunderstandings this time. Everything spelled out."

Lowering her gaze, she said, "About sex, you mean?"

Holden blew air through his teeth. Then he turned and paced away. "I'd better get the bacon. I hope you're hungry."

She wasn't, but that didn't seem to matter. By the time she had dragged on the robe, and hauled herself into the bathroom to brush her teeth and run a comb through her hair, he had a full-blown breakfast set out on the dining room table. Hash browns and hotcakes and bacon and eggs. A breakfast fit for a heart attack.

He pulled out her chair, and she sat down. Then he refilled her coffee cup before taking his own seat.

"Wow," she said. "I didn't know you could cook."

"There's a lot about me you don't know."

She nodded. "So, go on, will you? With...what you were saying before. About...terms."

Holden closed his eyes. "This is not easy for me," he said.

"No. Not for me, either. But I think it will be easier if you just lay it out on the table, Holden. Just get it said, and we'll take it from there."

He nodded. "Okay. That's what I'll do then."

She looked at him, waiting. He delayed the inevitable by filling his plate, but when he'd finished, he looked down at the food as if he'd lost his appetite.

"Holden..."

"All right, here it is. I am attracted to you. It was unfair of me to try to tell you I didn't want you, because I do."

She nodded. "Well..."

"I guess I didn't need to say that at this point. I pretty much let that bull out of the barnyard last night, didn't I?"

Her cheeks were heating, but she managed to nod.

"So, uh, this would be the point where you say something similar to me," he said.

She looked up from her empty plate, where she'd been staring hard enough to burn holes for a full tick of the clock. "You already know I want you, Holden."

"It might have been the wine."

"It wasn't."

"Okay. Okay, so we've established that. So here's the thing. I... I am not—" He bit his lip. "I'm not a one-woman man, Lucy. I'm not husband material. I'm not the kind of guy who would be good for any decent lady to settle down with or fall in love with or anything like that.''

She nodded. But she didn't want to look at him just now, so she started putting food on her plate to avoid having to.

"I married you to get my inheritance. That's all. And once I do that, this thing will be over. I don't want there to be any misunderstandings about that. I don't want you to go thinking—or hoping—for anything different.''

Again she nodded. "And you thought I would assume that if we had sex, that signaled some sort of change of heart," she said slowly. "You were afraid I would start hoping for something…ridiculous. Like a real relationship with you or, God forbid, a real marriage." She lifted her head, at last, and met his eyes. "Holden, you've done everything but hold up a neon sign telling me that isn't going to happen. Trust me, I believe you.''

He sighed, his shoulders slumping forward in relief. "Good. I just… I don't want to end up hurting you again.''

"Don't worry," she said. "I'm not gonna let you.''

He nodded. Then he dug into his food without much enthusiasm. Ate for a few moments. Lucy did likewise, though she wasn't much hungrier than he seemed to be.

Then she lifted her head, sipped her coffee to wash down her food and said, "So where does this leave things between us?''

He met her eyes, chewing, brows lifted as if he didn't understand the question.

"Regarding sex," she said.

Holden choked on whatever he'd just swallowed, reached for his coffee, and slugged enough of it down to clear his throat. Then he finally drew a breath and leaned back in his chair, staring at her.

Lucy told herself not to be embarrassed, but she was anyway. Still, this was necessary. Her life was on the line, as well as her only chance at ever becoming a mother. This was important to her, dammit. More important than her pride or her morals or anything else.

When he got hold of himself, Holden seemed to be searching for words. Finally he found some. "Look, Lucy, I don't think sex between us is a hell of a great idea."

She lowered her head.

"But…"

She looked up again. "But?"

Holden looked completely baffled. "Look, I'm not gonna kill myself trying to play the martyr here. I'm no saint, Lucy. And I'm not made of stone, either."

She shook her head at him. "You're saying?"

"I'm not going to initiate anything. Because I think it's a mistake. I think you're going to end up wanting more from me than I can give, and getting hurt."

She nodded. "But if…I'm the one to initiate things?"

"After everything I've just said, you would still want to?"

"Holden, we have to stay married for a year. I just don't see why we can't let ourselves…enjoy it."

He slanted her a glance. "You're saying…you enjoyed it last night?"

"What, you didn't pick up on that when I was screaming your name?"

He licked his lips, and she could almost see him remembering.

"I have to tell you, it was a far cry from the first time."

His brows went up. "That bad, was it?"

"Worse." She smiled, but let it die when he searched her eyes again. "Holden, if I were to tell you that I still want you..."

He closed his eyes. "Like I said, I'm not made of stone."

Smiling just a little, she nodded. It was going to work. She was going to get pregnant. Have a baby. Of her own.

And remembering last night, thinking about how Holden had been with her, made her realize that the process of getting what she wanted wasn't going to be an unpleasant one. In fact, just sitting here discussing it with him was making her temperature rise and her body grow moist and hungry.

She pushed her plate away, got to her feet while Holden looked on. Time to seal the deal. Once more for good measure. She had to be sure. "I have a deal of my own to offer you, Holden."

He looked scared to death. "Wh-what would that be?"

"Make love to me again. I'd like to try it once when we're both sober. And after that...I'll leave you alone."

He closed his eyes. "Lucy..."

"Holden, you're the one who just laid it all on the table. And this is me, initiating things."

"I don't understand you at all." He got to his feet, though, closing his hand around hers.

She lowered her head. "Holden... I'm not all that...experienced. And the few times I have...been with a man...I never—I mean, he couldn't make me..."

Holden's eyes slammed closed so hard and so fast she knew he understood what she was getting at. At least this much hadn't been a lie. He shuddered visibly.

"I like what I felt with you last night, Holden. I want to feel it again. And if you still don't understand me, then—" she parted the robe, and let it fall slowly down off her shoulders to pool on the floor around her feet "—then maybe this will help clarify things for you."

"Holy mother of... Lucy...." His eyes said it all. He backed away from the table, to come around it to where she stood, and he moved so jerkily that he knocked his chair over and didn't even seem to notice. And then he stood in front of her, his gaze raking her body as fire came to life in his eyes.

He was hers. Reduced to a trembling, totally erect slave willing to obey her every wish. And she knew it. It was kind of thrilling, actually, to realize that he was this powerfully attracted to her, when for so long, she'd believed him indifferent.

And as he wrapped his arms around her, pulled her close against him, as his hands and his mouth went to work eliciting sensations she'd never known before, she thought maybe she wouldn't keep her promise to leave him alone, after this. Maybe that was a promise she didn't want to keep at all.

Nine

Lucinda Brightwater Fortune was not turning out to be at all what Holden had expected her to be. He'd thought she would be the way he'd always thought of her. Far above being overwhelmed by anything as earthy as sexual desire. He'd thought she would be cool, cold even, in the physical sense.

She wasn't.

When he made love to her it was like nothing he'd experienced before in his life, and he had experienced a lot. She was hot, and hungry for him, and so responsive to his every touch, his every kiss, his every whisper. He hadn't realized he'd married such a firecracker. But he had. And when she told him she hadn't felt these things with any other man she'd been with, he was inclined to believe her. Maybe that was partly because it was good for his ego to believe her. And maybe it was just because he knew it was the same for him.

What the hell he was supposed to make of that, he didn't know. He just knew that if she wanted him, he didn't have the strength to refuse her. He'd tried to be honorable and do the right thing by her, but he'd never claimed to be a saint.

It was late morning by the time he got around to putting his clothes on and headed outside to survey the damage from the storm the night before. There were a couple of trees down. One of the trees had snapped the line from the generator to the house on its way. At least neither of them had hit the car when they'd come crashing down. And the driveway was still clear. He couldn't stay here indefinitely, but he could clean up the mess. He headed back inside to get what he needed.

"How bad is it?"

Holden looked up at the sound of her voice. And when he saw her, he got an odd little shiver up his spine. She was like two women. Right now, she was Lucinda in the Sky again. Clean, a white cotton shirt tucked into her jeans, her still damp hair pulled back into a ponytail. She had that fresh, girl-next-door face on again. And he could hardly believe she was the same woman who'd clawed his back and panted hot words into his ear this morning.

She looked as if she'd showered. He puzzled over that for a moment.

"The lake," she said, reading his face. "I went down and washed up there while you were out surveying the damage. So, how bad is it?"

Damn. He would have liked to have gone with her, naked, into that cold water. Damn.

"Uh, not too bad. There are a couple of trees down. I need to grab the chain saw out of the back room and clean up the mess."

"You want some help?"

His brows went up. "You want to help?"

She nodded. "I'm kind of eager to get back. Want to check in on that preemie and his mother."

Holden lowered his head. "I'm sorry we have to

spend the morning like this. I'd hoped we could talk. Get to know each other a little better before we headed back."

She averted her eyes. "I kind of thought we had."

"Yeah, well, that's not what I meant."

She nodded, lifted her gaze, looked slightly reluctant. "Well, we can talk while we work."

"Okay. I'll get that saw."

She wouldn't have expected him to power up a chain saw and attack a fallen tree like a seasoned lumberjack. She would have expected him to get on his cell phone and call for help, maybe order up a crew of blue-collar men to come and take care of this mess. She would have expected him to fix things up with his checkbook, not with his hands.

And his arms, and his shoulders and...

She was glad the chain saw made talking pretty much impossible. She didn't want to get to know him any more than she already had. She was afraid of that. She hadn't acknowledged the reason why, but it was in there just the same. All she wanted from Holden Fortune was a baby, and the money for her clinic, and to be allowed to keep right on seeing him as the kind of man he seemed to believe he was. A womanizer, a cad, a rogue just like his father.

She didn't want to learn otherwise. Because if he wasn't a total bastard, then what she was doing was really horrible.

But he was. Hadn't he agreed to have sex with her as long as she didn't expect any feelings along with it? No decent man would say something like that.

Anyway, it didn't matter.

She tore her eyes off him as he worked, wearing a tank top now that revealed way too much of him for comfort. Lucy picked up the fireplace-size chunks of wood he sawed away from the tree, and stacked them in the woodpile near the front of the cabin.

She tried very hard not to keep looking his way. And she also tried not to remember what it had been like to make love to him...last night, and then again this morning, and then *again* this morning, and—

Hell. She'd expected it to be quick and clinical. No more intimate, really, than artificial insemination would have been. He was just a sperm donor, after all.

But it hadn't been like that at all. He played her the way Mozart played the piano. He made her body come alive, her nerves sing, her heart thunder. He made her wish—

Oh, no. She wasn't going to fall into that trap. No. Uh-uh.

She piled more wood.

The sound of the chain saw finally died away, and Holden began helping her pick up logs and stack them. She glanced at the fallen tree. All the big parts had been cut into manageable hunks, and the smaller, bushy limbs laid all over the place.

"Now we can talk," Holden said, grinning at her as he brought a stack to where she stood near the woodpile.

She shrugged, and her nerves kicked in. "About what?"

"About you. I told you a whole lot about my family last night, so I figure it's your turn."

"Oh." She thought a second. That wouldn't be so bad. She couldn't learn anything too deep about him if she were the one doing the talking, right? Not that she really suspected there was anything all that deep to learn. He was just what he seemed. "Well…let's see. What do you want to know?"

Side by side, they walked back to the driveway, their arms loaded with wood. It smelled good, the mingled scents of chain saw exhaust and sawdust and the wood itself.

"What made you decide to become a doctor?"

She went still for just a moment, then straightened with her arms loaded down. "My mother."

"She encouraged you?"

"She…died when I was twelve."

"Oh, hell. I'm sorry, Lucy."

"It's all right. It was tough, but I got through it. It was ovarian cancer. When I started studying medicine I realized there had been warning signs. If enough had been known back then, they might have been able to prevent it."

Holden's eyes were on her, soft and sympathetic. "Matthew's mother died of cancer, too. I'm pretty sure that's why he took up medicine."

She nodded. "It's not an uncommon motivator."

"So what were these warning signs you mentioned?"

Shrugging, Lucy carried her logs to the pile, and unloaded them one by one. "She had a lot of trouble conceiving, which is why I'm an only child. I imagine there were precancerous cysts even then. If someone had caught on, diagnosed them soon enough…" Another shrug, and a sigh.

"Then, what?"

"I don't know. The sane thing would have been to

have her ovaries removed. But I'm not sure she'd have done it. She wanted another child very badly."

"But she wouldn't have died trying. Would she?"

Lucy brushed the sawdust from her hands. "She might have. The maternal urge can be pretty powerful, you know."

He frowned, and she didn't like that look, so she hurried back to the wood scattered on the ground, to pick up some more.

"It must have been tough on you, losing your mom when you were so young."

"It was."

"And what about your dad? He must have been there for you, helped you get through it, huh?"

Lucy shook her head. "Not really. Dad kind of withdrew into his grief after Mom died. He was there but he wasn't, you know? He was sort of…disconnected. Distant. It was like he shut down emotionally."

"In what way?"

More wood. Another trip to the pile. "Well, he stopped feeling. He didn't get mad, or sad or happy or anything. He just seemed to hover in some state of…nothing."

"So you aren't close to him anymore."

"No. I mean, I pay the obligatory visits at Christmas and Father's Day. He calls on my birthday. But there's not much of a bond there anymore. Once Mom was gone, we just grew apart. He moved to Dallas right after I left for college."

"That's really sad, Lucy."

She lifted her chin, forced a smile. "Sure a far cry from your family, isn't it?"

"Yeah. Sometimes mine are too close and too involved."

"I got that impression at our, uh, wedding."

"Logan? Hell, he's got chivalry coming out his ears. Probably thought you needed fair warning, and he'd be the only one noble enough to give it to you."

"I suppose his intentions were good."

"Yeah, well, they usually are. He doesn't exactly approve of my life-style. None of my family does."

Her lips pulled tight. Holden's gaze was too sharp, too attentive, and he noticed. "What?" he asked.

"I was just thinking how disappointed they'll be when they realize this marrying and settling down routine of yours was all a sham."

He shook his head. "You're probably right. But we'll have plenty of time to worry about that later."

She shook her head. "It's still kind of mean to get their hopes up. Maybe you should tell them the truth."

"Are you kidding? They'd crucify me."

"You're exaggerating."

"No way. You should have heard them all warning me away from you at the party. You're far too nice a girl for the likes of me, and they all know it."

She shook her head, a little wave of guilt rising up inside her. "They don't know me at all."

"They know enough. I agree with them on that."

"Oh, Holden, don't be—"

"And if they knew I'd somehow convinced you to go along with this scam, they'd be furious. Hell, I wouldn't blame them."

She looked up fast. "Doesn't anyone give a grown woman credit for having the ability to make up her own mind and face the consequences?"

He grinned. "They're mostly of the opinion that even a grown woman is helpless against the snake-in-the-grass charm of Cameron Fortune's firstborn son."

Her brows went up. She almost smiled. "Guess I'll be the one to prove them wrong then, won't I?"

He nodded, but she saw the doubt in his eyes. And she felt her own doubts creeping into her heart.

When the wood was all piled, they dragged the smaller limbs and scraps down near the lake, and piled them there. Holden said they'd make for a nice bonfire once they'd had time to season, and Lucy had a moment of anticipation when she'd actually felt herself looking forward to coming back here with him, sitting beside the lake in front of a roaring fire. It would be...

It wouldn't happen. And it would be a mistake to start thinking about future times, future visits, future anything. She had no future with Holden. She had to remember that.

When the work was done, they returned to the cabin, tidied the place up and packed their things. And by lunchtime, they were ready to head back to the real world. Her interlude with Holden was over. And she had to admit to herself that she'd relished every moment of it.

Holden wasn't worried. He knew his mother wouldn't let him down. She never had. He and Lucy stopped for lunch at a dirt-road diner they found on the way back home, and once they'd ordered, he excused himself to head to the bathroom. But instead he headed outside, where he leaned against the slab-sided building with a view of its single gas pump, and called home.

Mary Ellen answered the phone.

"Hi, Mom."

"Holden? Good Lord, son, where have you been?"

"Out at Lake Kingston. Listen, um, something happened. I would have liked to have talked to you about it first, but so much was going on...."

"Yes, it has been crazy here."

"Is there any word on the baby yet?"

He heard his mother's sigh, could picture her eyes clouding with worry. "No. Not a thing. Sam is doing all he can, but—"

"Sam?"

"Sam Waterman," she said.

Holden never had cared much for the way Uncle Ryan's head of security looked at his mother. The woman was a widow, for crying out loud. And hearing her refer to Waterman by his first name made Holden's hackles rise just a little. Made no sense, he realized. Hell, as lousy as Cameron had treated her, she'd certainly been faithful the whole time he'd been alive. She'd done her time, earned her happiness.

But Sam Waterman? Hell, she could do better.

"So, what is it you want to tell me?" his mother asked, breaking into his thoughts.

Holden sighed. "I guess there's no way to do this except to just come out and say it. I, um... I got married."

Silence. Absolute stunned silence.

"Mom?"

"Holden Cameron Fortune," she said, and he knew he was in for it. She never used his middle name unless she was furious with him. "If you think for one minute that you are going to bring one of those tramps of yours into this house...into this *family*—''

"I married Lucy Brightwater."

Again silence. Then, "Claudia's doctor?"

"Yes."

There was a long, slow sigh. "Oh, Holden. Oh, Holden, tell me this isn't some kind of game you're playing with her. She's such a sweet girl.... Holden, do you love her?"

"I married her, didn't I?"

"That is not an answer."

"Look, I'm calling from the middle of nowhere, and Lucy's waiting. I just wanted to let you know. We're on our way home now, and I think it would be nice if the family would...do something to show Lucy she's welcome."

A long pause. "That's...awfully thoughtful of you," his mother said, which he figured was her way of saying, "That's totally unlike you, Holden."

"I just want her to be comfortable with us. She hasn't had any family around her in a long time, and I think it would mean a lot to her."

"Of course it would. All right. I'll see what I can put together. What time should I expect you?"

"By seven, I imagine."

She sighed again, into the phone. "Holden...we're going to have a long talk, you and I. Soon."

"I expected as much."

"Be good to her, son. She's not the kind of girl you're used to. She's...she's a lady."

"I'm well aware of that. But I have to say, I'm glad you are, as well." He turned to peer through the smudged window, and saw Lucy sitting alone at the table. The waitress was bringing their food. "I have to go, Mom. Let me just run through what I'd like waiting for her, and then I'll have to go. I'll see you tonight."

"Yes. I'll see you then. Don't worry about a thing, Holden. I'll take care of it."

"I knew I could count on you," he told her.

"Always," she whispered.

She was, Lucy told herself, an idiot. Just because the pretty, big-haired waitress was ogling Holden openly, and just because he had been gone for so long, and just because she had reappeared only moments before he had, did *not* mean the two of them had been making out in some storage room somewhere.

So why was that what she was thinking?

Holden sat down, smiled. "Sorry I took so long. Had to make a call."

"That's all right." It wasn't, but it should be. She had no business keeping tabs on his every move.

The waitress appeared at once, to refill his coffee cup, and her smile was wide and sexy, and her eyes were suggestive and riveted to him. "Is there anything else I can get for y'all?" she drawled, including Lucy with her words but not with her eyes.

"I'm fine, thanks."

"You sure are, sugar." She winked, and sauntered away, her big butt swinging all the way across the diner until it vanished behind the counter.

Holden was good. He didn't even watch her go. Pretending not to notice the flirting, he dug into his food, sipped his coffee. But Lucy noticed. Every few moments she glanced across the room to see that hungry woman's eyes on him. And she was getting madder by the minute.

It was stupid. It made no sense whatsoever. And she felt it anyway. Jealousy. Blazing hotter with every sidelong glance.

"Something wrong with your sandwich?" Holden asked her.

"It's fine. Why?" She dragged her gaze away from the woman to focus on him. There was not even a hint of guilt in his eyes. Well, maybe that was because he didn't feel any.

"You haven't touched it," Holden said. "I'll send it back." He lifted a hand. "Hey, waitress?"

"Holden, no, I told you it's fine." But Big Hair was already wiggling her way back over here at the speed of light.

"What can I do you for, hon?"

Lucy rolled her eyes. Holden's gaze slid from Lucy's to the waitress's, and back again. "You sure the sandwich is okay?" he asked Lucy again.

"Yes. It's perfect."

Holden shrugged, and smiled up at Big Hair. "Never mind. False alarm."

"No trouble at all, sweetie." She'd pulled her pen out of her hair, in preparation to write down his wishes, Lucy supposed. Now, she dropped it. Deliberately dropped it. And when she bent to pick it up, her blouse gaped open revealing cleavage of Grand Canyon proportions.

The fury spilled over. Before she could even try to reason with herself, some crazy woman took over Lucy's body, and she lifted her hand, and bumped her water glass. It tipped, and the ice water splashed right where it should, soaking that big hair until it went flat.

The waitress shot to her feet with a squeal.

"Oh, my goodness! I'm so sorry," Lucy said.

The waitress yanked off her apron, and used it to dab at her hair.

"I really do apologize," Lucy went on. "Are you all right?"

She finished dabbing, eyed Lucy with malice, but then caught Holden's glance and calmed herself down. "That's all right, hon. It's only water."

She gave her apron a shake, then tied it around her waist again. "Can I get you anything else before I go get the mop to clean this up?"

"Yes, actually, you can," Lucy said, a sweet-as-light smile on her face, her voice sugarcoated. "I'd like some more coffee. That is, if you're done waving your chest underneath my husband's nose now."

The woman's eyes widened. She snatched Lucy's cup away and stomped off, muttering under her breath.

Lucy sighed, feeling an immense satisfaction…until she glanced Holden's way and saw him sitting there, staring at her as if he'd never seen her before today.

She licked her lips, growing nervous. "I shouldn't have done that. I've got no right to stop you from flirting if you want to."

"Um, yeah, you do, actually. We have an agreement. And for the record, Lucy, I wasn't flirting. She was."

She studied him, wondering what he was thinking.

Slowly, a grin spread across his face. "You're just full of surprises, you know that, Lucy?"

She shrugged. Actually, no one had been more surprised by her actions than she had been. What the hell was happening to her? It was as if this emotional, sexual, jealous woman had been hiding deep inside her all her life, never making a peep until now.

And now she wouldn't shut up for a minute.

Ten

When Holden pulled into the driveway at the house, Lucy was swamped with a mingled mishmash of feelings and memories. She couldn't help but recall the time long ago she'd been here before, with Holden. He'd been drunk and she'd been in the throes of teenage adoration. She'd lost her virginity, and later, her pride. He hadn't even remembered.

The other feelings were nervous ones. She had to face his mother. Together, she and Holden would tell the woman that her son was married. That she, Lucy, was her new daughter-in-law. Mary Ellen Fortune was a kind woman, but strong, and protective of her own. And Lucy wouldn't blame her in the least for resenting this hasty marriage, and the fact that she hadn't even been a part of it.

It wasn't going to be a pretty scene.

She was as prepared for it as she possibly could be. Holden had taken her to her own apartment first, and she'd taken a quick shower, brushed out her hair until it gleamed, applied a light coat of makeup, and donned a chic suit of deep sapphire blue. She felt a bit stronger than she would have felt facing her new mother-in-law dressed in jeans and a T-shirt, her hair in a ponytail. She'd also checked in on Cleo who was in the care of a neighbor and none the worse for wear.

When they pulled to a stop, Holden got out and hurried around to her side of the car. He opened her door, took her hand, smiled down at her. "Nervous?" he asked.

"A little."

"It's okay. I'm on your side, remember that."

She studied his face, his smile, the warmth in his eyes. He'd been so worried about her feelings toward him changing if they became sexually intimate. But if anyone's attitude had changed, it was his. He was more attentive, more...gentle with her, than he'd been before.

She let him tug her to her feet and was surprised when his hand closed around hers as they started up the walk to the huge front porch. But then she stopped and pointed. "Holden, why are all those cars in the driveway?"

He glanced toward the fork in the drive, where several vehicles were lined up. Shrugged. "There are always lots of vehicles here. Employees and stuff."

She frowned at him. "They must be well-paid employees."

Again, he only shrugged, and quickened his pace, drawing her up the front steps. He paused at the door, sent her a funny little smile, and then opened it and pulled her inside.

The house was pitch-dark. "All those cars, and the place looks deserted," Lucy whispered. She wasn't sure why she was whispering.

"Oh, I'm sure *somebody's* home. Come on."

He pulled her on, through the dim foyer, and into the gargantuan living room she remembered so well.

And as soon as he flicked on a light, a chorus of voices yelled, "Surprise!"

Lucy blinked in shock. A dozen Fortunes, maybe more, stood there smiling at her. Beyond them, she saw gleaming balloons bobbing in the air, anchored in place by long curling strands of ivory ribbon. There were several stunning arrangements of white roses placed around the room and a mound of gaily wrapped gifts piled on a table at one side.

"I—I don't know what to say," Lucy stammered.

Mary Ellen Fortune came up to her, her eyes warm and welcoming. She reached out to enfold both of Lucy's hands in both of her own. "Welcome to the family, Lucinda. My lovely new daughter."

Lucy's heart surged up into her throat. Her eyes filled, and the warmth of Mary Ellen's hands seemed to reach all the way to her soul. "You...can't know how much what you just said means to me, Mrs. Fortune."

Mary Ellen's brows went up. "Of course I do. And you're to call me Mary Ellen...at least until you feel comfortable enough to call me Mother."

One of Lucy's hands pressed to her chest, as if to calm the erratic beat of her heart. "Thank you."

"Don't thank me, thank your husband dear."

Blinking, she turned to look up into Holden's eyes. "You did this?"

"I just called ahead—" he began.

"Holden's too modest. He was determined to make sure everything would be perfect for you when you arrived." She lowered her voice, leaned closer. "He must care very deeply for you, Lucinda."

Lucy just nodded, battling tears still. She wanted to

turn to Holden, wanted to thank him, or hug him, or… But Mary Ellen was pulling her into the crowd of family members, all of whom welcomed her with a warm embrace, or a kiss on the cheek, or a kind word. Claudia was there, and so was Matthew, both of them looking drained and exhausted. Claudia hugged her gently. "We can't stay, darling. But we wanted to be here when you arrived, and wish you well."

"I'm so glad you were. Thank you, Claudia." Lucy glanced up at Matthew. "Has there been—"

"Not yet. But it won't be long now." His voice was strained, and tiny lines of tension bracketed his mouth where none had been before. "Bryan will be safe in his mother's arms before we know it."

"I know he will," Lucy said.

"We don't want to stay away from the Double Crown for very long," Claudia said. "In case there's…any word."

Lucy knew it would make little difference if they were at the ranch house, or here, a mere two miles away. But she understood that need to be close, to stay very near the last place they'd seen their beloved child. "I don't blame you a bit. Go on. I promise, I'll visit you there soon."

Claudia nodded, her eyes damp and painfully red as her mother-in-law guided her away, and toward Holden, who remained near the door, watching.

Logan appeared, repeating his offer to help her if she needed it. She wasn't certain just what kind of help Logan thought she might need, but she thanked him for the offer.

Holden's uncle Ryan gave her a hearty hug, and Lily welcomed her with a shadow in her eyes. Lucy remembered Lily's warnings about Holden, and she knew the woman probably thought she was crazy to have married him.

Vanessa smiled, saying she knew it all along. "I could see there was a spark between you two, even with all that was happening at the christening."

Lucy said nothing, and fortunately Holden chose that moment to reappear at her side, his arm sliding possessively, protectively, around her shoulders. He leaned down close to her ear. "Overwhelmed yet?"

She smiled up at him. What overwhelmed her was that he had called ahead to set all this up.

Mary Ellen led them all to the formal dining room where a huge dinner awaited. And when they'd finished eating, she rose, the picture of grace. "One last surprise, Lucy. If you think you can bear it."

"Another surprise?" Lucy looked at Holden. He looked back, a knowing smile playing with his sexy mouth. "You again?"

"This one was my idea, yeah. I thought…well, it wasn't much of a wedding. And you deserve more, so I, um…" He shrugged.

"Bring it in, ladies."

The double doors at the far end of the dining room opened and a cart was wheeled in. Atop it, the most glorious wedding cake Lucy had ever seen towered, layer upon layer, stacked with white pillars in between. Pristine white icing and delicate flowers and vines and even a pair of lighted taper candles decorated the creation. And at the top, two white china doves, nestled together beneath a lacy arch with real bells dangling from it.

Lucy couldn't breathe. She rose from her chair without even realizing she'd moved, and went closer to the confection. It was perfect. Perfect in every possible way. Her heart swelled...and yet it ached, too. She felt like a fraud. Everyone had gone to so much trouble to help her celebrate a marriage that wasn't even real.

Her tears spilled over this time. She couldn't hold them in. She looked toward Holden, her gaze locking with his. He got slowly to his feet, came toward her, and picked up the ribbon-decked cake knife. "Shall we?"

"It's too beautiful to cut," she whispered.

"We took plenty of pictures of it, dear," Mary Ellen told her. "And we'll save the top layer, of course. You can't cut that until your first anniversary."

Their first anniversary. Maybe they'd eat it to celebrate the divorce. Lucy met Holden's eyes, and knew he was thinking the same thing. Why did the idea hurt so much?

She closed her hand with his around the knife handle, and together they poised it over the cake. "Make a wish," Holden whispered.

And she closed her eyes and wished with everything in her that this dream was real.

Then her eyes flew open. A baby, she thought frantically. I meant to wish for a baby.

But the blade was already sinking through the cake and the family was clapping their hands and cheering.

Holden took Lucy to his wing of the house when she started looking as if she'd had enough. The party had gone on for a couple of hours, even after the cake was served. Drinks, snacks, family chatter and coffee, the usual Fortune family chaos.

He hoped she'd liked it. He thought she had.

He guided her through his wing, showing her the small, private kitchenette, and the living room, the tiny office he kept here for those rare occasions when he had to work from home, the large bathroom with its sunken, whirlpool bath, and finally, the bedroom.

Their bedroom.

"Um…I can arrange things so you have your own bed. I'll do that tomorrow. I should have thought—"

"You thought of everything, Holden. That was really sweet, what you did for me." She sank onto the edge of the bed, looking tired, maybe a little weepy.

"It was too much, wasn't it? I shouldn't have had them all here to—"

"No." She lifted her head, met his eyes. "It's been a long time since I've had…a family around me."

"I know. That's why I thought you'd like this."

"I did like it. I just don't think I'm clear on why you did it."

Holden frowned, tilted his head. "I—I don't know. I mean, I wanted to do something nice for you." He tried a tentative smile. "Is there a clause in our agreement that I can't do nice things for you?"

She closed her eyes. "No. It was nice. And I'm grateful. I just…" She shrugged. "I never realized you could be so thoughtful."

He shrugged. "Well, now you do. Surprise."

She averted her eyes. Seemed nervous. As if she were avoiding looking at him. Finally she got to her feet. "I'm going to take a shower. It's late, and I have to be at the hospital early in the morning."

Ah, so that was it. No sex on her mind tonight. Maybe she was overwhelmed by his family after all.

Or by him. Or maybe she felt odd sleeping with him in the house with other people around, though they were all so far away it couldn't possibly matter. And no one would bother them.

She turned toward the bathroom. He caught her arm. "Wait a minute."

She faced him, her eyes wary.

"Lucy, you don't think I'm...expecting anything, do you?"

Lifting her brows, she pretended not to know what he meant.

"You do, don't you? Lucy, just because you and I had sex at the cabin doesn't mean I'm expecting you to be all over me now that we're back here. Don't feel like you're under some kind of...pressure here."

She blinked, apparently surprised again. "Then it's...it's all right with you if we don't—"

He lifted a hand, touched her cheek. "Of course it's all right with me. And you don't need to make excuses, either, Lucy. Sex wasn't part of our bargain. I don't ever want you to come to me for any other reason than because you want me."

She blinked. "I... You..." Then she sighed, shook her head. "You're not the man I thought you were, Holden."

"Yeah, well, you've given me a few revelations, too, lady." He smiled at her, threaded his fingers in her hair and gave it a playful tousle. "Go take your shower, Mrs. Fortune. You can wear one of my T-shirts to bed. And tomorrow we'll get the rest of your stuff packed up and shipped over here, if that's okay with you."

She nodded. "Okay," she said.

It was later, when she went to sleep in Holden's bed and he lay in the next room on the sofa, making sure she didn't feel any kind of pressure, that the guilt rose up again. Not a small wave this time, but a big one. What the hell did she think she was doing here? Holden Fortune was pretty obviously not the man she had believed him to be. Oh, he was convinced, it seemed, that he was just like his father. Thoughtless, selfish, obsessed with sex and women and cheating on his wife.

But Holden was different. That was becoming more and more obvious to her. All the years she'd spent telling herself she hated him, blaming him for everything that had happened to her...they made no sense now. No sense at all. And tricking the man into getting her pregnant suddenly seemed wrong.

She wasn't sure she could go through with it now.

Damn him. Why did he have to turn out to be such a decent, caring man after all?

"Where is Lucy?" Mary Ellen asked when Holden came into the breakfast room for his morning coffee. He could have had a cup in his own little kitchen, but when he'd awakened to find Lucy already up and gone, he'd been lonely. And even though he knew what was likely awaiting him, he'd decided to face the music and have breakfast with his mother.

"She had to be at the hospital early this morning."

"Oh? Well, that's all right. Gives us a chance to have that talk I promised you."

"Mother—"

"Holden. I know why you did this. Or at least why *you* believe you did this."

He frowned at her, his filled cup in one hand, the coffeepot in the other. "Why I believe I did what?"

"Married Lucy, of course. You believe you married her so that you could inherit your share of your father's estate. And don't deny it, Holden. I know you better than you know yourself."

Holden took a deep breath, prepared to argue with her, then let it out, seeing in her sharp gaze that she did, indeed, see right through him.

"Sit down, Holden."

He set the pot down, pulled out a chair, and took it. "Don't lecture me on this, all right? Lucy and I are both adults, and we both know what we're doing."

Mary Ellen nodded. "Then she knows your reasons for marrying her?" She searched Holden's face, but he didn't admit or deny a thing. "Well, that's a relief. At least you didn't deceive her into this. I assume she had her reasons for agreeing, though I can't imagine why a woman like Lucy would marry for anything less than love."

She waited, brows lifted high.

Holden hated the way she had of getting to him, making him spill his guts when he had no intention of doing so. "She needs funding for an obstetrical clinic to care for low income women."

"I see."

She was looking at him again. Just looking at him.

"Look, I'm not going to let her get hurt in this thing. I'm well aware she's not the kind of woman I have any business being with, and—"

"She's exactly the kind of woman you should be with, Holden."

He blinked, scratched his head, and looked at his mother. "What?"

"She's perfect for you. A lady, Holden, a far cry from the trollops you've been dating as you continue on this endless search of yours for...for whatever it is you've been trying to find. Don't you see?"

Slowly, Holden shook his head. "No. No, I don't see. Look, I'm like my father. You know that. I'm a no-good—"

"Be careful, son. I loved your father."

"And suffered your whole life because of it. You think I'd put Lucy through that kind of hell?"

"No. You wouldn't."

"Damn right, I wouldn't. She's special, Mom. She's...she's good and she's clean and she's...she's like you. She reminds me of you."

Mary Ellen bit her lower lip, and her eyes began to water.

"Oh, come on. Don't..." Holden got up, went around the table, and hugged his mother gently. "Don't cry. I didn't mean to make you cry."

"Then don't say such sweet things to me, son." Lifting her head from his shoulder, she looked him hard in the eyes. "You're nothing like your father, Holden. I know. I lived with the man, and I've raised you. I know you as well as I knew him, inside and out, and I am telling you, you're *not* like him. You're afraid you are, you believe you are...but you're not."

He sighed deeply. "Hell, I wish I could believe that." He straightened away from her, returned to his seat, picked up his cup and sipped his coffee.

"I remember when you were in high school. You talked about Lucinda once or twice. I remember the way you looked whenever her name came up. Like a child longing for a candy that was up high, on a shelf he couldn't reach. I knew then that she was special to you."

"No, Mom, I think you're letting your imagination run a little bit wild on you."

"You fell in love with her way back then, didn't you, Holden? But you convinced yourself you weren't good enough for her. Didn't you?"

He shook his head, denying every word of it, but his gut ached and his chest felt tight.

"If Lucy had asked you to fund that clinic," his mother went on, "would you have agreed to it? Even without this…this marriage agreement?"

Meeting her steady gaze, he nodded.

"And don't you think she knew that?"

"No. She seems to be amazed every time I do anything even the slightest bit decent for her. I'm sure she never would have thought I might back her clinic without getting something for myself in return."

Mary Ellen frowned. "I think you're underestimating her. She's a smart woman, Holden. Sharp. I think she could have asked you for that money, and had it. And I know she could have asked Ryan, or Matthew and Claudia, or even me, and we'd have helped her fund this thing. And I think she knows it."

Holden set his cup down carefully. "So what are you getting at?"

"She married you, Holden. But not because she had to. She could have had her clinic without resorting to such drastic measures. So, logic would dictate, she must have had some other reasons for agreeing to such an outrageous proposal."

His mind was filling with questions. Thanks to his mother. God, this had all been so simple before. Now it was getting more complicated by the minute. "What other reasons could she possibly have had?"

His mother shrugged. "Maybe, Holden...she loves you, too?"

"Now wait a minute!" Holden was on his feet again. He stood so fast he sloshed coffee on his hand, and then he slammed the cup down and sloshed some more. "That's ridiculous. She knows me, she knows what I'm like. Hell, after what I put her through in high school, she all but hated my guts. No, Mom, there's no way in hell—"

"What you put her through in high school?" his mother asked, her delicate brows lifting as she took a sip of her favorite tea. Chamomile. Must be her secret for always being so calm, so cool, so damned poised.

"Never mind. That doesn't matter."

"Oh, everything matters, dear."

"No, it doesn't." He paced away, paced back again, shoved a hand through his hair. "She's not in love with me. She's not going to fall in love with me. She's going to be my wife, on paper, for a year, and then she's going to take her money and leave."

Mary Ellen set her china cup onto her saucer with a deliberate precision, got slowly, gracefully, to her feet, and folded her arms over her chest. "Holden."

He stopped pacing, turned to face her.

"I like her. She fits in this family. She is *exactly* what you need. And she is most certainly staying."

Holden felt under attack. His brows went up. "What do you mean, she's staying? Look, she and I made an agreement and—"

"You love her, Holden."

"I don't—"

"You love her."

"I'm fond of her, yeah, but I don't—"

"Holden, darling, stop fighting so hard. Listen to your heart, not your head. You're in love with the girl. Now get over yourself, swallow your pride, and set about making sure she feels the same."

Holden closed his eyes and sank into his chair, feeling as if his legs had turned to jelly.

"And, Holden?"

"What?"

"That's an order, sweetie."

He opened his eyes. His mother sent him a sly wink across the table, an encouraging smile, then she got to her feet and left him alone.

"She's wrong." Holden looked at his coffee, but didn't drink it. It didn't hold any appeal all of a sudden. "She's dead wrong," he told the cup. "I don't love her. For God's sake, if I loved her I wouldn't have told her at least a dozen times that I didn't, that I never would, that things between us were going to be totally unemotional. Would I?"

The coffee cup didn't answer. Instead, the brew inside gleamed with a reflection of his own stunned, stricken face, and mocked him with it.

"Oh, hell," he whispered. "I think I love her."

Gina Gonzales stood arm in arm with her husband, her palm pressed to the glass, her face damp with tears, when Lucy came up beside her. She looked in at the row of pink-skinned newborns in their plastic bassinets, and past them, at the incubator that held

Gina's premature daughter and the tubing running from the newborn's IV pole to her body. So tiny. So fragile.

Lucy put a hand on Gina's shoulder. "Her doctor says she's doing better today."

Gina nodded, her eyes never leaving her child. "*Sí.* He told me so this morning. But still, she is so little, compared to the others."

"She'll grow, Gina."

Gina nodded.

"Have you named her?"

A slight smile, and Gina managed to glance Lucy's way for a moment. "She is named for you, Lucinda."

"Oh my...." Lucy was so touched she didn't know what to say. "Thank you. I'm honored."

The child's father nodded firmly. "She is strong. She will be well."

"Yes, she will," Lucy agreed. "Gina, I wanted to talk to you. You can go home today."

Gina's eyes widened as she turned to face Lucy fully for the first time. "Without my baby?"

Lowering her head, Lucy said, "She needs to stay. It's for her own good, Gina. She needs to be stronger before we can let you take her home."

"But I cannot leave her!" She turned to her husband and he put his arms around her, held her close.

"Dr. Brightwater, you cannot make my Gina leave our baby behind. I will find some way to pay you, but I—"

"No. No, wait a minute. You both misunderstand me completely. Listen, come and sit down, let me try to explain."

Reluctantly, the couple let her lead them down the

hall and into her office. She poured coffee for them from the pot she kept in the corner, handed them each a cup, then perched on the edge of her desk.

"Now, first things first. Gina, you are well, healthy and strong. I couldn't keep you here even if you were a millionaire. It has nothing to do with your income, only with the fact that I can't fill hospital beds with healthy people when there are so many others who need them. Other women, having babies, who need to rest and recover afterward. You wouldn't want me to have to turn them away, just so you could use a hospital bed you don't need, now would you?"

Blinking her eyes dry, Gina shook her head.

"You can see your baby as much as you want. Stay with her all day every day if you want to. No one is going to restrict your visits."

Lowering her head, Gina said, "But I cannot. We live on the other side of town, Dr. Brightwater. There is only the pickup. Miguel needs it to work and—"

"Then stay here, near the hospital. There are motels and—" As soon as Gina's eyes met her husband's, Lucy knew she was way off base. They couldn't afford that, either. She pressed her lips together. Getting personally involved was a big no-no, but in this case...

"How long will little Lucinda have to be here?" Miguel asked.

Lucy shook her head. "It depends on how she does. But it's going to be at least another week. Possibly two."

Gina lowered her head and sobbed softly. Miguel looked pained, and pale. "How will we ever pay for this?" he muttered.

"We have programs, financial assistance for low

income families.'' Lucy got up, turned to rummage through the mess on her desk for the applications. She finally found them and handed them to Miguel.

He only held up a hand and shook his head. "I have seen these before. I make more at my job than those papers say I can make. We do not qualify for this assistance of which you speak.''

"I was afraid of that.'' Lucy lowered her head, shaking it slowly. It was a trap she'd seen all too often. Patients without insurance, their meager income a bit too high to qualify them for aid, a shade above abject poverty. But that was still too little to give them any hope of paying their hospital bills. She knew this baby's hospital stay could spell financial ruin for its family.

"All right. Listen, I can help you with part of your problem." She went around her desk, opened the big bottom drawer, and pulled out her purse. Then she extracted a set of keys, took one off the ring and, carrying it to Gina, pressed it into her hand. "I have an apartment, not far from here. Actually, it's within walking distance.''

Gina frowned, looking confused.

"I...just got married, and I'm living in my husband's home now. There's no reason you can't use the apartment until the baby is released. All right?''

The two looked at each other, eyes widening. "You...you would do that for us?''

Lucy smiled and went back to her desk, grabbing a pen and a notepad. "Here's the address," she said. "It's not hard to find. Go to the end of this street and turn right. Second building on the left. Apartment

10-C. Okay?'' She tore off the sheet and handed it to them.

Gina took it in a trembling hand. Then she came around the desk and enfolded Lucy in a hug. "God bless you, Dr. Brightwater.''

Lucy smiled and hugged her back. "Now, why don't you go back to your room and get dressed while I get your release forms in order, hmm?''

"*Sí, sí*. I will. Thank you.''

The two got up, looking at least a bit more hopeful than before, and hurried out of her office. And Lucy stood in the doorway, watching them. It felt good to have brightened their lives just a little bit. But there was so much more they needed…so much more so many families on the far side of town needed. And a week or two in her apartment wasn't going to make a hell of a lot of difference in the long run.

She sighed, and turned to go back into her office.

"Lucy?''

Looking up, she saw Holden coming toward her, a bag in his hands. And she smiled a welcome in spite of herself. "Hey, aren't you supposed to be at the office or something?''

He shook his head. "Executives get to take long lunches when they want to.'' He held up the bag. "Doctors don't, though, but I thought you might be able to tear yourself away long enough for some take-out.''

"You're a mind reader. I was just debating whether to go hungry or brave the hospital cafeteria.''

"Guess that makes me your knight in shining armor, then.''

She stepped aside and waved him into the office.

He set the bag on the clean spot at the edge of her desk, then quickly scooped her papers and folders into neat stacks and set them out of the way. Lucy stood back, arms folded over her chest, watching him. "You're good at this."

"You ain't seen nothing yet, Doc." Holden opened the bag and produced a tiny bud vase with a single white rose in it. Lucy's brows went up. "Leftover from last night's festivities," he said, setting the little flower in the middle of her desk. Then he tugged containers of food out of the bag, placing them on the desk one by one, followed by paper napkins, plastic eating utensils, and a pair of paper cups with covers firmly in place. Finally, he pulled two chairs up close to the desk, held the back of one, and said, "Your table is ready, Dr. Fortune."

She shook her head, and took her seat. "You don't do anything small, do you, Holden?"

"Hardly ever." He took his own seat.

Lucy opened the lid on her cup and saw whipped cream dusted in what smelled like cinnamon. "Cappuccino?" Curious, she lifted the lids on the containers of food. She'd been thinking burgers and fries, but suddenly she doubted that was the case.

Chicken Kiev, glazed asparagus, and some kind of chocolate confection that smelled as good as it looked, stared up at her. She picked up one of the containers, turning it until she saw the name of the restaurant blazoned on the side. "Lombardi's? You brought me takeout from the best restaurant in town?"

He shrugged. "You didn't eat much at the party last night, and this morning you skipped out without any breakfast."

"And how do you know I didn't stop at a fast-food joint on the way?"

He shook his head. "Fast food is unhealthy. Besides, you were in too much of a hurry to check up on that preemie. How is she, by the way?"

"Past the crisis point. Healthwise, at least. Looks like she's going to be okay."

Holden smiled. "I peeked in at her on the way up. Looks like a fighter to me."

Lucy felt her brows draw together, and she tipped her head to one side. She never would have suspected Holden to have cared one way or the other about that baby. In fact, she would have thought he'd have forgotten all about it by now. But he'd actually gone by the nursery to peek in at the child?

Who the hell was this guy? He sure wasn't the Holden Fortune she'd known. Or the one she'd *thought* she'd known.

She dug into the food, which was heavenly. "This is great, Holden. It was really sweet of you."

"I had another reason for being here."

"Oh?"

"I promised to get your stuff moved in today, remember?"

She blinked, gave her head a shake. "I thought that meant you'd be sending some movers to take care of it."

"I did. They're meeting me at your place in—" he glanced at his watch "—thirty minutes." He shrugged. "I just didn't think you'd want strangers going through your stuff, unsupervised. Besides, I want to personally pick up the beast you call a cat. So I'm..."

"Supervising?"

He grinned. "Guess that would be the word for it."

"Well, don't be surprised if you find a couple in the apartment when you get there."

Holden frowned. "You sublet it already?"

"No. I loaned it out. To that little preemie's parents. They needed a place to stay...ah, it's a long story. At any rate, I told them they could use the place until the baby's released."

Holden stared at her for a long moment.

"You don't approve?" she asked.

"I... You're so *good*. You know that? You amaze me."

She felt her face heat, and looked away. "I just wanted to help."

He was still looking at her when she faced him again. But he sighed, gave his head a shake, and finished his meal. She really didn't know what to make of Holden Fortune anymore. She'd thought of him in the same way for so very long, and now it seemed every day brought a new and unexpected revelation.

"So, did you like your lunch?" he asked when nothing remained but the empty containers he was even now tossing into the wastebasket.

"It was the best lunch I've ever eaten at this hospital. I'm not used to so much pampering, Holden. You're going to spoil me."

"Yeah, well, that's the plan." He offered her a small, oddly shy smile. "You're a Fortune now, Doc. Might as well get used to a little pampering."

He got to his feet, and she walked with him to the door. But he hesitated there, shifting his weight from one foot to the other, and not quite meeting her eyes.

"Hell," he said, and then he leaned down and brushed a kiss across her lips, turned and hurried away.

Lucy stared after him in abject confusion. What the hell was that all about?

An RN passed by, sent Lucy a wink. "New boyfriend?" she asked.

"New husband," Lucy replied. "Totally new."

Eleven

Just as Lucy had said he might, Holden found Miguel Gonzales at her apartment. What he did not find was the moving men he'd hired.

Miguel offered his assistance, as well as his pickup, and the two of them spent the afternoon packing and loading Lucy's belongings, and her cat, trucking them out to the house, and then unloading them again.

Miguel turned out to be a strong son of a gun with ambition to spare, and it made Holden think. The guy wasn't lazy. He wasn't stupid, either. But he had been born into poverty, and raised in it as well, and it seemed to have had its claws into him before he ever had a chance. One bad break after another. But he was a fighter, same as Holden had pegged his little daughter to be. And he was determined to get past it.

"It's hard," Miguel said as he packed knickknacks from the living room into boxes, wrapping each one in newspaper first. "I took the first job I could find, but it was only part-time, so, no insurance. Then I find a second part-time job, and then a third, but again, part-time, no insurance. The bosses, they work me all the hours they can, but refuse to put me on as full-time help. Because then they would have to pay more in benefits for me."

"It ought to be criminal," Holden commented. He

was in the next room, Lucy's bedroom, folding her clothes into boxes. It was a bit tough to concentrate on what Miguel was saying every now and then, when he'd find himself holding some scrap of an underthing in his hands, feeling its silk, thinking of Lucy.

"Meanwhile, I work so many hours there is no time to go out looking for a better job. And if I take time off to do so, I don't get paid. I cannot afford to miss a single day's work. I was lucky to be able to get away for the birth of my daughter and to visit her today in the hospital." He sighed loudly.

Holden tugged another item out of Lucy's dresser, and began to fold. Then he noticed the photo on the dresser. Lucy, probably about eleven years old or so. Standing in between her father and her mother. Looking happy, carefree.

"Your wife...she is a good woman, Señor Fortune," Miguel said slowly. "It would have hurt my Gina deeply not to be able to see our baby every day. But the doctor, she knew that."

"I know she's a good woman." Holden stared at the photograph, thinking not long after it had been taken, she must have lost her mother. And how painful that had been for her. How painful it still was.

And her father was out of her life too, for all intents and purposes.

She was good, and kind and caring. She didn't deserve all the unhappiness she'd seen in her life.

"You know she's going to set up a clinic out near where you live," he said, just to make conversation.

"She is?"

"Yeah. One people can afford to use. Pregnant women, babies, all that stuff."

Miguel came to stand in the doorway, and when Holden looked up, it was to see his eyes were filled with admiration. "Do you know what that will mean to our women, Señor Fortune?" He shook his head slowly. "I think this wife of yours, she is some kind of angel."

Holden smiled widely, and his chest literally felt as if it were swelling with pride. "She is, isn't she?" Amazingly, she was so good that she made him want to be better. For her.

Two days later Lucy was running late at the hospital again, and feeling especially guilty since she'd promised to go to the Double Crown for dinner with her husband and his family tonight. Holden didn't deserve this. He'd been so sweet since he'd brought her home. On the couch, every night. Not a complaint about her sudden loss of interest in—

"Running late again?" he asked.

"I'm so sorry, Holden," Lucy said into the receiver. "I didn't intend to be here this late, it just—"

"Don't apologize. You're a doctor. That's what you do, and doctors have strange hours. It's fine."

He was being so damned nice. It was one thing to go ahead with her plan to get pregnant when she thought he was a jerk, but when he was this sweet all the time... Hell, she didn't know which was the real Holden Fortune. The thoughtful, caring man she'd married, or the rogue who'd stolen her virginity all those years ago?

"I really wanted to go over to the Double Crown with you tonight."

"You will. I'll wait for you."

"Oh, but I don't want to hold you up."

"But you don't want to walk in there alone, either."

She smiled at his perceptiveness. He had a way of knowing almost exactly what she was thinking so often it was getting uncanny.

"Meet you in an hour, then?"

"I'll be here. And, Lucy?"

"Yeah?"

"Don't go driving fast or anything stupid like that, okay? If you're late, you're late."

"Thank you, Holden."

She heard the click as he hung up the phone. She replaced the one on her desk, sat there a moment, and just shook her head. What if he really was this sweet man he seemed to be? What if...

She closed her eyes, licked her lips. She wanted to make love to him again. And not just to get pregnant. What the hell was wrong with her?

A tap on her office door brought her out of her thoughts, and when she went to answer it, she found Gina Gonzales standing there, smiling at her.

"I don't know how I will ever repay you," the woman said, and she wrapped her arms around Lucy and hugged her tight. "But I promise you I will find some way."

Lucy accepted the hug. "Gina, really. It's no big deal. The apartment was just sitting empty anyway and—"

"Oh, but I am not talking about just the apartment!" Gina backed off, and looked up at her, smiling. Then her smile faded. "You mean, you do not know what your husband has done?"

"My...husband?"

"*¡Sí!* That man of yours, he has given my Miguel a job at his company!"

Lucy blinked. "He...did?"

Gina nodded hard. "With good pay. And insurance, and he even fixed things so the hospital bill will be paid." She shook her head slowly. "I thought he would have told you all of this."

"No," Lucy said. "No, he didn't say a word."

"You thank him for me," Gina said, smiling. "You tell him my Miguel will be the best worker he has ever had."

"I'm sure he will."

Gina turned to hurry back to the nursery, leaving Lucy standing there dumbstruck. Damn. Okay, then. That sealed it. Holden Fortune may have been a total jerk once. But he wasn't that anymore.

And it would be wrong of her to trick him into getting her pregnant. Dead wrong. So she couldn't very well go back to sleeping with him....

Oh, but what if he still wanted to?

Stupid question. What she really meant was, what if *she* still wanted to. And it wasn't even a question, really. She *did* want to. And it was a mistake, and she knew it, and she wanted to anyway. Hell, why did he have to be this way? She would have been perfectly safe if he'd only been the bastard she'd believed him to be. Perfectly safe.

But she wasn't safe. Her heart wasn't safe, and her body had already surrendered to the other side.

With a sigh, she gave up. She wanted him again. She also wanted a baby, but that was going to have to wait now. She'd just have to take her chances. It wasn't fair to use a decent man the way she'd planned to use Holden.

She grabbed her purse, locked her office door, and headed out of the hospital. She'd figure all this out later.

Somehow.

Holden was waiting for her on the front porch when she got home that night. Looking too good to be legal. Relaxed, sitting in the porch swing, and wearing a pair of snug-fitting jeans, a Western shirt with pearl snaps, a belt with a big fat buckle, and even boots.

Lucy felt herself smile when she saw him sitting there, waiting for her, his eyes warm and attentive. It felt good having something to come home to besides an empty apartment and a fistful of impossible dreams.

Holden rose slowly, reaching out a hand to take hers. "You look beat," he told her. "Sit down for a minute."

She eyed the porch swing longingly, but shook her head. "I should shower and change. We're already late—"

"So we'll be a little later. No one's gonna be upset. Come on." He tugged her, until she sat in the swing. Then he went to the wicker stand and poured iced tea from a dewy pitcher into a tall glass. He brought it back, pressed it into her hand, and sat down beside her. "Tough day?"

She took a long pull from the glass, and it seemed to cool and refresh her inside. Leaning her head back, finding his arm behind her for a pillow, she closed her eyes. "I had to tell a fifteen-year-old girl that she was pregnant this morning." She shook her head slowly. "Things didn't get any better from there."

"I'm sorry." He sighed slowly. "What's she going to do?"

Lifting her head, opening her eyes, Lucy found herself surprised he would ask. But less surprised than she would have been the day before. "I don't know. I had a long talk with her and her mother, tried to explain all the options to them. But...well, they'll need some time to think it through."

Holden nodded. "And you'll lose sleep over it until they decide." She frowned at him, but he just shook his head. "Don't bother denying it. You care about these people. Maybe a little more than is healthy for you, Doc."

"You should talk," she said quickly.

It was Holden's turn to frown. "What's that supposed to mean?"

She took another drink, and set the glass down, turning toward him in the swing. "I had a visit from Gina today. She told me what you did for Miguel."

"Oh." Holden shrugged, averting his eyes. "It wasn't that big a deal, Lucy."

"Oh, no? It changed their lives, you know. I'd call that a big deal."

He sighed. "I like the guy. We met and got to talking when I moved your things from your apartment. Thought he deserved a break, and hell, if I can't give a decent man like Miguel a leg up, then what's the point in running Fortune TX at all?"

She stared at him for a long moment. "You are a decent man, Holden Fortune."

"You say that like it's a surprise."

"It is. All this time you've had me thoroughly convinced that you were as shallow and self-centered as...as those bimbos you date—"

"Used to date," he corrected her gently. Then he looked away, drawing a deep breath, lifting his chin. "And you were right to believe that. Because it was true. If I've changed then it's your fault."

"My fault?" She tipped her head to one side, watching his face. His jaw was tight, and she sensed he wasn't just making conversation here, but speaking from somewhere deep.

He nodded, meeting her eyes. "You are so good. You make me want to be a better man."

Inexplicably, her eyes grew damp, and she averted them to hide the fact. "That's...a really sweet thing to say."

"It's the truth. Since you've been around I've...I don't know, been seeing things a whole lot differently." He shrugged. "I've even started thinking maybe I'm not so much like my old man, after all."

His gaze was practically searing her skin, and her mind was jumping all over the place trying to interpret those words. She didn't want to read him wrong. It scared the hell out of her, and she got to her feet, not knowing how to reply or even how to feel. "I should go get ready."

"Okay. Make it casual, Lucy. I thought maybe we could go riding after dinner."

She paused in the doorway. Horseback riding, around the sprawling Double Crown. It would be romantic, and they would be all alone. And she wanted him. So how was she supposed to deal with that?

* * *

Lucy looked like a million dollars, and Holden tried
for a second to imagine walking into the big, rustic
dining room at the Double Crown with any other
woman on his arm and feeling the way he felt right
now. But he couldn't. Lucy was one of a kind. She
wore her hair loose, and it gleamed, as black as mid-
night, and moved with her. Even in her jeans and
white silk blouse, and a pair of ankle-high suede boots,
she looked like royalty. She wore blue jeans the way
Audrey Hepburn or Jackie O would wear them. You
couldn't hide that inborn grace beneath clothes. It
would shine through if she wore a feedbag, he thought.

It was an intimate dinner, not the whole clan tonight, and that was good. Uncle Ryan and Lily were
there, along with Matthew and Claudia, and Dallas,
Ryan's youngest son, and Vanessa, one half of the
Fortune twins.

"I'm so sorry we're late," Lucy said the second
they entered the room. "It was my fault. I got tied up
at the hospital."

"Don't apologize, Lucy," Lily said quickly.
"We're all aware how important your work is. And
while dinners can wait, babies can't."

"That's true enough." Lucy smiled, and the others,
who'd been milling around snacking on hors
d'oeuvres, took their seats. Holden pulled out Lucy's
chair for her, and then took the one beside her.

The first thing Lucy did was reach across the table
to cover Claudia's hand with her own. "How are you
holding up?"

Claudia lowered her eyes. "Just getting through one
hour at a time, though they seem endless."

"I know."

"Any new developments since I spoke to you last?" Holden asked his cousin.

Matthew shrugged. "No, nothing."

"Actually," his father said, clearing his throat, "there is one bit of news to report. I had a call from the FBI today." Everyone looked toward Ryan, and Holden could almost feel Matthew and Claudia holding their breath. "They're sending in a top-notch special agent to take over the investigation. Fellow by the name of Devin Kincaid."

"And that's *good* news?" Vanessa asked, her voice as soft as always.

Ryan looked at her, frowning. "Why wouldn't it be?"

Shrugging, Vanessa sighed. "I just think we're going about this all wrong. Everyone's looking for clues and evidence, looking at dollars and cents, waiting for the kidnappers to make a move." She shook her head. "What we ought to be doing is getting inside the kidnappers' heads, figuring out why they took Bryan away, what's motivating them."

"Money is what's motivating them, little sister," Dallas said softly.

"Maybe not. Maybe there's something more."

"And maybe your being a shrink is influencing your thinking," Dallas chided, his tone teasing, but with an underlying seriousness.

"I'm not a shrink, big brother, I'm a psychologist studying for my Ph.D. And I've worked in the field of criminal psychology enough to know what I'm talking about. You get some by-the-book, hard-nosed, federal type in here, and God only knows how far back he'll set things."

"Vanessa..." Dallas began.

"I think she might have a valid point," Lucy said. "So, Vanessa, maybe you should just ride herd on this Fed, make sure he covers all the bases."

"That's exactly what I intend to do," she said, not sounding at all like her usual soft-spoken self. Holden guessed where her precious nephew was concerned, Vanessa could be a real lioness. He almost pitied the poor FBI fellow, whoever he was.

"I don't care whose methods work, so long as we find my son," Matthew said, sighing.

"I know." Holden met his cousin's eyes. "I never realized just how precious a child is, until now. Seeing both of you makes me think how I'd feel if I had a baby of my own and someone tried to take it from me." He closed his eyes, gave his head a shake. "But it won't be for much longer. Hell, the world isn't big enough for them to hide Bryan from us for long."

"You got that right," Matthew said, and he reached across the table to clasp Holden's hand, looking as if he was challenging him to arm wrestle. When he let his hand go again, Matthew said, "I never thanked you for what you did that night at the party. I was... I was over the edge."

"No big deal," Holden said.

"You, too, Lucy," Matthew added, nodding toward her. "You really came through." He smiled a little. "I think you're good for this family. You've got steel in your spine."

"She'd have to have, wouldn't she?" Dallas asked, sending Lucy a wink.

Everyone laughed, though there remained an uneasy tension just below the surface. Rosita brought the food then, and the family settled into eating. Holden noticed Lucy's sharp gaze on Claudia and Matthew, and knew she was watching to see if they ate, or just made a pretense of it.

After dessert, while they all sat in the great room sipping coffee, Holden said, "Dallas, I'd like to take Lucy riding tonight. Show her around the spread. Is that okay?"

"Fine by me. You an experienced rider, Lucy?"

She shrugged. "I have ridden. But I'm no expert."

Dallas nodded. "I'll call down to the stable and have a pair saddled up and ready for you. A nice gentle mare for Lucy. And something a little more challenging for my cousin, I think."

"No, Dallas. I'll take a gentle mount, too," Holden said. "This ride is for relaxation, not adventure."

Dallas's brows went up, but he shrugged. "Calming down in your old age, are you?"

"That's what marriage does to you, little cousin," Holden replied as he smiled wickedly and winked at Lucy.

Twelve

Lucy looked just as good on the back of one of the finest quarter horses in all of Texas as she did anywhere else. In diamonds or denim, his bride looked at home, comfortable, as if she belonged.

Maybe that was because she did.

"So, how big is this place, really?" she asked, her head turning one way then another as she scanned the horizon. The rolling green fields, dotted with longhorns in one direction, horses in another, crisscrossed by lush hedgerows and smooth, clean fence lines.

"The Double Crown? Five hundred thousand acres, give or take."

"Good God, that must be half of Texas."

Holden smiled at her. "Damn near. Double Crown longhorns are known as the best Texas beef to be had, and the horses have a reputation all their own that's growing every day." He patted the sleek neck of the horse he rode as he spoke. "Don't you, girl? Yeah, worth your weight in gold."

Lucy laughed. "You like them. The horses."

"Grew up with 'em. Oh, I don't have the knack for running the ranching end of things that Dallas has, which is why I'm head honcho at the corporate offices of Fortune TX, and he's in charge here."

"But you miss it, I'll bet."

"Didn't think so, until recently. I thought I was pretty content with life in the fast lane. But I'm gonna start spending a lot more time here. Hell, what good is being the boss if you can't knock off early and go riding when you feel like it?"

"Healthy outlook."

"It feels right."

They rode alongside a field where longhorns grazed. Each movement like something done in slow motion, the big, lazy animals emitted a sense of peace, of calm.

"Here's a good spot," he said after a time of riding in comfortable silence.

"A good spot for what?"

He sent her a smile. "Don't worry. I didn't bring you up here to ravage you." She averted her eyes when he said that. "Is that a look of relief or...disappointment, Doc?"

Now she looked alarmed. "Holden, I—"

"No. I'm sorry. I shouldn't have asked you that." He slid down from the saddle, looped the reins over a low-hanging limb, walked to Lucy's mount, and reached up a hand. "Come down for a minute. I want you to see something."

"All right." She let him help her down. His hands clasped her waist, and remained there for a long moment after her feet touched the ground. He looked down into her eyes, before he forced himself to let her go. But he couldn't resist taking her hand in his as he led her around to the far side of the little knoll where they'd stopped.

When he sat down in the grass, she sat down beside him. He didn't think he'd ever wanted a woman the way he wanted her. But he wasn't going to push her.

"Look," he said, and he pointed to where the sun rested on the horizon in the distance. "The sunsets are incredible from here."

"Wow." She leaned back on her hands, and watched the brilliant ball of fire slowly dip lower, and lower, sinking deeper behind the distant hills with every passing moment.

The sky around them turned from blue to dusky purple by gradual degrees, and she said nothing the whole time. Just sat there watching it all, and he sat there, watching her.

After a long while, when the sky was almost dark, and the sun gone from sight, she said, "I ought to tell you something, I think."

He waited, wondering what was on her mind.

"I know you must be pretty confused by my behavior since we got married."

Holden shrugged. "You don't have to explain yourself to me, Lucy."

"No, I think I do. At the cabin I was... And since we got back, I've been..." She gave her head a shake. "Sex is...well, it's a complicated issue for me."

"I know that. I'm largely to blame for that, in fact. It's okay."

"It's not that I don't want you," she blurted all at once.

When he didn't answer, she looked at him, searching his face in the gathering twilight. "I'm glad to hear that," he said slowly. "Because I want you pretty badly, you know. Not pushing here, just wanted to be sure we were clear on that."

She bit her lip, lowering her eyes. "I'm glad you told me."

"There's no hurry, Lucy. Whenever you're ready. To tell you the truth, I've got a few puzzles of my own to work out."

"Do you?"

He nodded, reached out and smoothed a lock of her hair behind her ear. "Yeah. I do. See, I always thought I knew exactly what I wanted out of life. Thought I knew who I was, what I could be, and what I couldn't. But all of that is mixed up now. Like I took all the components I thought were me, and tossed 'em in a sack and shook the hell out of them. And there are some new ones in there that I can't even identify yet." He shrugged. "I do know I'm changing the way I see a lot of things. And I think I like myself a little better now than I ever did before."

She smiled quickly, and averted her eyes to hide her grin.

"What?" he asked her. He caught her chin and gently turned her to face him again. "What's that grin about?"

She shrugged. "I was just thinking I like you better now than I ever did before, too."

"Yeah?"

She nodded. But then her smile died. "I'm changing, too, Holden."

"Not too much, I hope."

Drawing a breath, she sighed. "You're always going on about what a—a good person you think I am. But I haven't been. Not really. Holden, I've done some things that would make you change your mind about me in a hurry."

He frowned, certain she was imagining things. "I don't believe that's possible."

"Well, it is. I'm far from perfect."

He shrugged. "Perfection is overrated."

"Anyway, it's over now. Holden, I don't know what sort of marriage this is going to become over the next twelve months. But I do know this. It's going to be honest. From now on, okay?"

He frowned more deeply at her, a tiny ball of worry forming in his stomach. "Are you saying it hasn't been up to this point?"

"No. Not entirely."

He took a deep breath, stiffened his spine. "You want to tell me what it is you've kept from me, then?"

She shook her head. "Not tonight, Holden. But I will. Soon. I promise."

He studied her for a long time, finally sighing and giving in. How bad could this secret of hers be? This was Lucinda in the Sky, for heaven's sake. She didn't have a bad or dishonest bone in her body.

"I can't make love to you tonight, Holden. I want to…I really want to, but I can't. I need to take care of some things first. But I'd really like it if…if you could just hold me. Will you do that?"

She didn't need to ask him twice. Holden's heart flip-flopped, and his bones seemed to melt, and he pulled her gently into his arms. When she rested her head on his chest, he stroked her hair. "I'll hold you all night long, if you want me to, Doc," he whispered.

And that was exactly what he ended up doing. Sharing his bed with her, holding her close, aching for more but knowing she wasn't ready. Trusting in her goodness enough to know she'd tell him whatever secrets she'd been keeping in her own time. And enough

to know, too, that they wouldn't be as bad as she
thought they were.

He was pretty certain he wanted to keep her with
him forever, if she'd have him. He was pretty certain,
too, that with Lucy at his side, he could be the kind
of man she deserved. Maybe he had been all along,
and just hadn't seen his true self. When he looked into
a mirror, he'd seen only his father's reflection. Cameron's son.

Now, he saw Lucy's husband. And he liked the
man.

Lucy didn't want to think that maybe Holden had
changed his mind about the nature of their marriage.
But that was what she was thinking, in spite of herself.
Maybe he'd realized the same things she had. That he
was a good, decent man, capable of anything he set
his mind to. Including a long-term commitment to one
woman.

To her.

Maybe she was a fool to get her hopes up. She only
knew she'd be an even greater fool to go on with her
initial plan. She had to give this relationship a chance,
and tricking the man into getting her pregnant was
killing any chance it might have.

So all her plans were on hold, and if things worked
out with Holden then she'd tell him she wanted a
child, and about her limited window of opportunity to
make that happen. And if things didn't work out with
him, then they'd go their separate ways and she would
look into artificial insemination and hope she hadn't
waited too long. All she knew was, right now, she
needed to step back from this plan. Slow down.

She still wanted Holden, and he wanted her, and that was so thrilling to her that she could barely contain it. But she was going to do this right. Get on some birth control first. She would pick up some condoms on the way home to use in the meantime, but she wanted something more reliable.

Which was why she'd come into the hospital a bit early this morning, and why she stood now outside the door of her friend, Susan Martinez's, office. She couldn't go to Karen Flemming for this. Knowing how badly Lucy wanted a child, Karen would have too many questions. Susan Martinez wasn't a gynecologist, but a general practitioner. Still, she'd help her out. Lucy was sure of it. Straightening her spine, Lucy knocked.

"Come in," Sue called.

Lucy stepped inside, offered her colleague a smile, and decided to plunge ahead without preamble. "I need a favor."

"Name it." Susan got up from her desk and crossed the room. "How's the new marriage going?"

"Amazingly well," Lucy said, which made Sue send her a quizzical glance. "Never mind that. Look, I need to get on birth control, Sue, but I don't want to get anybody up in arms over me writing my own prescriptions. It's been a sore subject ever since that physician's assistant got busted for selling all that Methadone."

"Not to mention strictly against hospital policy," Sue added. "And it's probably not a bad policy, at that."

"So, will you help me out?"

Sue tilted her head. "What about Karen? Isn't she your regular gynecologist?"

"She's got a full schedule today," Lucy said quickly, averting her eyes to conceal the lie. "And I'm in a bit of a hurry. Will you do it?"

Sue just shrugged and smiled. "Of course I will. What have you been using so far?"

"Nothing."

Sue blinked three times, opened her mouth, closed it again, and finally gave her head a shake. "You're a newlywed and you haven't been using any birth control?"

Lucy rolled her eyes. "I've only been married less than a week. Just give me a prescription and I'll—"

"No way. You know better, Lucy. Not without a physical first."

"Sue, you don't understand—"

"You're a doctor, Lucy. You should know better than to even ask. Look, let's do this right now. It'll be quick, I promise. Ten minutes, and you're out of here. Okay?"

Sighing, Lucy said, "Fine. If that's the only way."

"It is, and you'd be telling me the same thing if our situations were reversed. Come on across the hall to an exam room."

"Let's just make it fast, all right? I have rounds."

Sue smiled, and held the door open.

Lucy put her clothes back on a few minutes later, while Sue quickly scribbled on her prescription pad. "Like I said, just a formality. But you know, better safe than sorry." As she spoke, she glanced up at the test tube with the urine sample in it...and then she went very still.

"Sue?"

"Uh...well. That's interesting."

"What's interesting? Give me the prescription, so I can get out of here, will you?"

Licking her lips, Sue tore the sheet off the pad, held it up, and ripped it slowly in half. "Afraid not."

"Sue! What the heck are you doing that for?" Lucy jumped off the table, and bent to pick up the fallen, ruined prescription. "Is this supposed to be funny?"

Sue looked at Lucy, took a deep breath, and then pointed. "Maybe you'd like to take a look at this for yourself?"

"At what?" Lucy turned to look at the test kit that lay on the counter, and then she blinked and looked again. "No."

"Well, actually, that would be a yes."

"But I... That can't be right."

"No, must be a mistake. Having unprotected sex for a solid week couldn't possibly result in pregnancy. Where did you say you went to med school, Lucy?"

Lucy put her head in her hands, shaking it slowly, her mind whirling.

"We can do blood work to confirm, hon. But, uh, I'd say you're in no need whatsoever of any birth control pills." Sue put both hands on Lucy's shoulders. "Are you okay with this?"

"I...hell, I don't know."

"You want me to call your husband, have him come in and—"

"No!" Lucy clapped a hand over her mouth. "No, I... No."

"Okay. All right. Listen, you look a little thrown.

Why don't you go home, take the rest of the day off, and deal with this news?''

''My patients...''

''Karen and I will cover for you. Okay? Do this, Lucy. You look like you just got hit between the eyes with a mallet. Go home. You need time to digest this, obviously.''

Feeling as if she were in a daze, Lucy nodded. ''All right. Okay, I'll just...I'll just go home.''

Holden wouldn't be there yet. She could hide in their bedroom, and try to think. This was a dream come true, and a nightmare. She would have the miracle baby she'd prayed for, but probably lose the man she'd let herself fall in love with in the process.

Fall in love with? Who was she kidding? She'd been in love with Holden Fortune since she was a teenager. But this would end it. This would show him the devious sort of woman she really was. And then it would be over.

Over. Because if he cared about her at all, it was all based on the false image he had of her. He'd put her on some kind of pedestal. Thought of her as flawless and good.

Lucy pressed her palm to her abdomen. Tears flooded her eyes, and her knees felt watery and weak. ''What have I done?'' she whispered. ''Oh, God, Holden, what have I done?''

Holden whistled his way through the morning meeting at the plush offices of Fortune TX, Ltd. Logan had been sending him odd looks on and off, but Holden didn't really care. He was feeling good about himself, and good about his life for the first time in a long time.

He'd decided on a course of action, and just knowing what he had to do seemed to make his steps lighter and keep a constant smile teasing at his lips.

He was going to woo his wife. Court her. And make her fall in love with him. Because he could be the kind of man who would make a woman a decent husband. Hell, with Lucy at his side, he could do anything.

His brother followed him to his office when the meeting adjourned, and even that didn't upset him. Holden just filled his coffee cup, and took a seat behind his gleaming hardwood desk, tipped back his leather swivel chair and propped his feet up on the blotter.

Logan stood in the open doorway. Just beyond him, Holden saw Emily Applegate peering intently at her computer screen.

"How's that acquisition research coming, Emily?" Logan asked, without turning.

"Just fine," she said, looking at him and smiling. "It's on your desk."

Logan came inside and closed the door. "So, what's up with you, anyway?"

Holden lifted his brows, sipped from his cup. "What do you mean?"

"You're smiling. There's a bounce in your step. I actually heard you humming in the elevator, Holden."

"So?"

"So, you don't hum."

Holden shrugged. "Maybe I just started."

Frowning, Logan came forward, and sank into one of the two comfortable chairs in front of Holden's desk. "Something's different about you. It's Lucy, isn't it?"

Holden grinned. "I'm planning a surprise for her." Then his smile died and he bit his lip. "I just hope she likes it. I mean...I'm not really sure she will, but I think—"

"You're in love with her!" Logan said it as if it were an accusation.

"Well, she's my wife. I'm supposed to be, right?"

"I can't believe it." Logan was on his feet again, but his frown was gone. He was smiling now. "I honest to Texas can't believe it. Maybe you're not as dense as I thought you were after all, big brother."

"Runs in the family," Holden said.

"Huh?"

Holden shook his head. "Have you taken a good look at your assistant lately, Logan?"

Logan's face puckered in confusion. "Emily? No. Why, is there something wrong with her?"

"And you call me dense." Holden's phone buzzed, and he snatched it up, then put a hand over the receiver. "Mom's on the line. I'd better take it."

Logan nodded, frowning. Holden understood that frown. It wasn't like Mary Ellen to call either of them at the offices—unless something was wrong. He thought of little Bryan. Perhaps there was some news, and he prayed it was good. Holden punched a button on the phone panel. "Mom? What's up?"

She sighed first. "I probably shouldn't be butting in, Holden, but your Lucy just came home, and—"

"She came home?" He glanced at his watch. She couldn't have been at the hospital for more than an hour. "Did she say why?"

"Something about not feeling well."

"She's sick?" Holden was on his feet. "Is she all right? Maybe you should call a doctor."

"Holden, your wife *is* a doctor. Besides, I have a feeling it isn't so much physical as...as something else."

"What kind of something else?"

Another sigh. "Holden, she's pale, a bit shaky, and, um, if I'm not mistaken, she's been crying. Did something happen between you two that—"

"No. Hell, everything was going so well...or I thought it was. Look, I'll be home as soon as I can. I'm leaving now."

"Good," Mary Ellen said. "I think that's for the best."

Holden hung up the phone, glanced at his brother, having almost forgotten Logan was in the room. "I have to go—"

"I heard. Go ahead, I'll handle things here."

Holden nodded his thanks, snatched his keys from his top drawer, and headed for the door.

"Holden?"

"Yeah?"

"Work it out, okay? She's... Hell, she's one of the best things that ever happened to you."

Glancing back over his shoulder, meeting his brother's eyes, Holden said, "Wrong, little brother. She's *the best* thing."

The gentle tap on her bedroom door made Lucy lift her head from the pillows. It ached when she moved it. And she knew her eyes were puffy and red, and she didn't really want to face anyone right now.

"Lucy? Darling, it's Mary Ellen. Please, let me come in."

Blinking, brushing her eyes dry, Lucy got to her feet, and opened the bedroom door. Her mother-in-law stood there, looking like the epitome of motherhood—graceful, caring, wise. Perfect. She held the cat in her arms, stroking him absently. She and Cleo had become best friends, just as Holden had predicted they would. Mary Ellen was such an incredible woman.

"I can't believe Holden ever thought I was like you," Lucy whispered, turning her head, averting her eyes.

"He told you that, too, did he?" Mary Ellen came in and closed the door. "When he said it to me, that you reminded him of me, I thought it was the highest compliment I'd ever been paid."

A burst of air escaped Lucy's lips. "It was no compliment, Mary Ellen. I'm not half the woman you are."

"You are the woman my son loves," she said softly. Coming closer, she put a hand on Lucy's shoulder. "That makes you perfect in my eyes."

"He doesn't love me. He can't. He thinks I'm something I'm not, and I've been...I've been horrible. Oh, Mary Ellen, when he realizes what I've done..." Lucy closed her eyes to fight off new tears.

"Come with me, Lucy. I've got tea waiting in your sitting room. It will do you a world of good."

Lucy let herself be led. Mary Ellen tucked her into a cozy chair, draped a woven blanket over her shoulders, and then placed a cup of steaming tea into her hands. She felt comforted. It was almost like having a mother of her own again.

"Now, why don't you tell me about this horrible thing you think you've done?"

Lowering her head, Lucy said, "I—I deceived him, Mary Ellen. I was selfish, and thoughtless. I married him with a plan, with my own agenda, one he knew nothing about."

Mary Ellen nodded. "I assumed this arrangement began as a part of Holden's own agenda. To collect his inheritance."

Nodding hard, Lucy said, "It did. He promised to fund my clinic for the lower income women in the Hispanic and Native American communities in return for being his wife for a year."

"And you agreed," Mary Ellen said softly. "And now you've fallen in love with him."

Setting her teacup into its saucer, Lucy said, "It's so much more complicated than that."

"Well, now. Let me see if I can guess. I did have a rather interesting phone call from Rosita Perez this morning. Rosita is a bit of a psychic. Most of the family just humors her, but I've seen her pick up on too many things to be entirely skeptical. Rosita said she dreamed about tree frogs last night."

Lucy, distracted for just a moment from her misery by this odd twist in the conversation, sniffled, and looked up. "Tree frogs?"

"Oh, yes. You see whenever Rosita dreams of amphibians, someone in the family turns out to be pregnant."

Lucy's teacup clattered to the floor.

She stared at the spreading liquid, staining the carpet, soaking into its fibers bit by bit.

Mary Ellen gathered both Lucy's hands into her

own. "So, tell me, Lucy. Are you going to make me a grandmother?"

Lucy squeezed her eyes tight and managed to nod. She felt the hot tears seeping through despite her best efforts to hold them back. And then she felt warm arms around her, holding her gently, a hand stroking her hair.

"This is not the disaster you think it is, you know. It's a blessing, Lucy. A blessing." She backed up a bit, framing Lucy's face with her hands, and smiling. Mary Ellen's eyes were damp, too. "You're going to make such a beautiful mother. You know that?"

Lucy couldn't help it. She smiled, too, through her tears. "Do you think?"

Tears rolling freely now, Mary Ellen nodded. "If I could have chosen a mother for my first grandchild, I would have picked you." She closed her eyes. "Oh, Lucy, do you know how lively this old house will be? The birthday parties, and slumber parties and..." She drew a big breath, eyes flying wide. "And Christmas! Oh, Lucy, it's been so long since I've seen the wide, wonder-filled eyes of a child on Christmas morning."

Everything she said brought an image to Lucy's mind. And bit by bit, the anguish left her. Mary Ellen was thrilled for her, and it felt good to relish the idea of motherhood, to cherish the thought, and celebrate the beginning of a new life with this woman. But when she thought of Holden, the images faded. And the joy with them.

"Holden is not going to be as enthusiastic, I think."

"Holden will be thrilled, just as I am, Lucy. I promise you that." Mary Ellen took a breath. "I won't say anything to him. I'll leave that to you. You tell him when you feel ready, all right?''

"Thank you, Mary Ellen."

Mary Ellen nodded, getting to her feet. "No, Lucy. Thank you." Leaning down, she pressed a warm kiss to Lucy's forehead. "Now, go wash your face. Your husband is on his way home."

Lucy's head came up fast. "What?"

"I'm sorry. I was worried about you."

Nodding slowly, Lucy said, "It's all right."

"It's as it should be," Mary Ellen said. "I'm going over to the Double Crown for a while. You two will have the place to yourselves today."

Nodding again, Lucy forced a smile as Mary Ellen took her leave. Dragging herself to her feet, she retrieved the toppled teacup. Then she went to the bathroom to splash cold water on her tearstained face.

Thirteen

Holden hurried through the house, into their wing, worried half to death. Things couldn't go bad now. Not when he'd just figured out what he wanted in life.

He found Lucy in the bedroom, standing sideways in front of a full-length mirror, staring hard at her reflection.

"Honey? You okay?"

She looked up, startled, turning away from the mirror almost guiltily. "I was a little under the weather, so I came home early. Your mom really shouldn't have bothered you at work."

Holden took his time studying her face. Her eyes looked a little puffy, and there was a worried look about her that bothered him. "So...it's just some kind of bug?"

"Probably a summer cold." She sighed, and crossed the room toward him. "You really didn't have to rush home."

"I was worried. Mom thought you looked upset."

She lowered her eyes. Holden took her hands in his. "If I've done something to upset you, Lucy, you have to tell me about it."

She smiled, but it looked false. "You have been absolutely wonderful to me. I promise, it's nothing you've done."

"What is it, then?"

She pulled her hands from his, turning away. "Nothing. A bug, like I told you. You can go back to the office, and I'll be fine."

"No."

Blinking, she turned back to him. "Well...why not?"

"Because if you're sick, then I want to be here to take care of you. You know, prop your feet up, feed you chicken soup, get you tissues..."

"I'm not that sick."

"I don't think you're sick at all."

She closed her eyes when he said that, and he knew he was right. "Holden, I—"

"We're going to talk it out, whatever it is. I have some things to say to you. And maybe I should have said them sooner, but—"

"Holden, don't. Please."

He fell silent, studying her face, the hint of pain he could see in her eyes. With a sigh, he reached out, took her hand. "Come on." She didn't resist as he pulled her to the bed, pressed her until she sat on its edge. Then he dragged up a chair and sat beside the bed.

"Talk to me."

Taking a breath, letting it out slowly, she seemed to be steeling herself. She parted her lips. Then closed them again and sighed.

"Fine," Holden said. "I'll start. I want to call off our deal."

Her eyes widened. "Y-you what?"

"Oh, I'll still fund the clinic. Fully. No limits, what-ever you need. But...okay, I'm just gonna plunge in and say it. I don't want to end this marriage when the year is up.'' Leaning forward, he took her hand. "I want to try to make it real, Lucy. I want to try to make it work.''

"Oh, Holden." It was a whisper, a sigh. "You don't know what you're saying.''

"I know that I feel something for you. That I pretty much always have.''

"No," she said, her voice stronger now. Firmer. "You don't.''

Holden lifted his brows. "Give me some credit. I know what I feel.''

"But you don't know me." She got to her feet, pacing away from him in quick, agitated strides. "You think I'm perfect. Some kind of angel.''

"You are.''

"No, Holden, I'm not. I never have been. These feelings you think you have aren't for me. They're for some false image of me that you've built up in your mind. But that's not who I am.''

He couldn't help it. He smiled. "All these years I had myself convinced I could never be good enough for you. Now you're trying to tell me you're not good enough for me?''

She turned slowly. "Y-you thought you weren't good enough for me?''

"Yeah. That's why I stayed away from you. It was a battle, I can tell you that. But you seemed out of reach for a man like me." As she lowered her head, shaking it, Holden went to her, stroked her hair away from her face. "I always believed I was destined to be just like my old man. But you made me see that I'm better than that. I can be exactly what *I* want to be. You showed me that, Lucy. And what I want to be is your husband.''

He didn't know what he'd said wrong, but all of a sudden there were tears standing in her eyes.

''You were always good enough for me,'' she said. ''Holden, I lied to you, and plotted against you.''

He frowned, staring down at her. ''What?''

''I was dishonest with you from the start. I had my own agenda when I agreed to be your wife. A cold, calculated plan to get what I wanted from you. Because for some screwed-up reason I believed you were just a womanizing jerk who would never care anyway.''

He lowered his head. ''I...probably deserved that.''

''No. No, Holden, you didn't. You see, I was wrong. You were never the kind of man I thought you were. Never the kind of man you thought you were, either. I saw that almost from the start, and I knew then that I couldn't go through with m-my plan to trick you.''

Frowning, he searched her face.

''I swear, Holden, I changed my mind. I did.''

''So, then...there's no harm done.''

She sniffled, brushed at her eyes with the back of one hand. ''There is. Because you need to know the kind of scheming I did, and I just don't think you'll feel the same way about me anymore once you do. I think you care for the woman you thought I was. But that image is going to be shattered.''

Nodding slowly, Holden lifted her chin until she looked into his eyes. ''Only one way to find out,'' he said, knowing full well that no confession she might make was going to make him feel any differently about her. "Tell me this devious plot you couldn't go through with. What was it? Were you going to sue me for divorce and try to take half of everything I own, the way Sophia is doing to Uncle Ryan?"

"No. No, it's worse than that, Holden." She licked her lips. "I—I wanted a baby."

He felt his jaw go lax, snapped it closed again.

"I wanted to get pregnant right away. And that was why I—I seduced you the way I did, at Kingston Lake."

Holden gave his head a shake. "That...that was why?"

She lowered her eyes. "Well, that was why the first time. I mean, I wanted you, Holden, don't mistake that. But...I wanted a baby, too. I've always wanted a child of my own, and my time was running short, and when you made your offer I thought it was the answer I'd been looking for."

Turning in a slow circle, Holden pushed both hands through his hair. "I can't believe this. I was... I was a damn sperm donor to you?" He stopped when he faced her again. "And just what were you planning to do with this...this baby?"

"Keep it. Raise it as my own. I wasn't even certain I was going to tell you about it. I thought I could leave town before I started to show, let our marriage go on until the end of the term we agreed on, and then get a quiet divorce."

"And when you came back to town toting a child? What then?"

She gave her head a quick shake. "I hadn't thought that far ahead. Claim I'd adopted it, maybe. I don't know. I guess I just didn't think you'd care, anyway."

"You didn't think I'd care?" Holden paced the floor, sighed deeply, and then brought himself to a stop. "Okay. Okay, so you had this plan. Hell, Lucy, you probably felt justified. You knew me as the guy who got drunk and took your virginity one night, and then forgot it ever happened before morning." He sighed again, bit his lip. "I guess the main point is, you changed your mind."

"No, Holden. The main point is, I am not this perfect, pure-of-heart Snow White you've come to think I am."

"If you weren't," he said, moving closer to her again, taking her shoulders in his hands and squeezing gently, "you would have gone through with it. But you didn't. That's why you didn't want to make love to me when we got back, isn't it?"

Eyes wet, she looked up into his and nodded. "By then I'd begun to see the man you truly are. I decided to wait, to get some birth control, and talk to you about children later. Once we figured out where...where this thing between us was going."

He smiled very slowly. "And we will. We will, Lucy. Much, much later."

She blinked up at him, wide-eyed.

"So, you're not perfect. Lucy, nobody's perfect. I never expected you to be flawless. I'm not perfect, either. You know that."

She sighed deeply.

Holden tipped his head back and shook it slowly. "Thank God, your little plan didn't succeed," he said. "God knows, a baby is the last thing we need in our lives right now."

She didn't reply. Didn't say a word, and when Hol-

den looked down at her, her face seemed frozen. A
mask he could not see through.

"I mean, there's so much going on. Sophia fighting
for half of everything, including the company. Little
Bryan's kidnapping." Her expression didn't change.
"We need time to figure out what there is between
us…time to nurture it, see if it grows. You understand
what I'm saying, don't you?"

Unflinchingly, she nodded. "Yes. I think I do."

"So, you agree. I mean, babies…that's something
for much later. Way down the road. I'm still adjusting
to the idea of being someone's husband, you know?
Being someone's father, well…"

"No, I understand perfectly. I'm—I'm glad we
talked this through, Holden. I am."

"Good." He sighed with relief. "So we can start
over, then?"

She lifted her head, looked him square in the eye.
"No. I'm afraid we can't."

Holden felt as if she'd just nailed him between the
eyes with a two-by-four. "What?"

She turned away from him. "I just… I'm not ready
for this. It's like you said, being someone's wife, it's
a big adjustment. I, um…"

"Lucy?"

"I need some time, Holden."

"Some time?"

She nodded hard. "I think I'll just move back into
my apartment for a while, and…mull all of this over."

"My God, Lucy, what the hell just happened
here?"

She kept her back to him, her head lowered. "I
didn't realize you were thinking of making this mar-

riage anything other than the arrangement we agreed to. Now that I know you are, I'm just not sure it's wise of me to stay here.''

"But...but I thought you... I thought you wanted that, too?"

"We just established that you don't know me as well as you thought you did."

Desperation clawed at him. Something had happened, something had changed here, and for the life of him he didn't know what. "You can't go back to your apartment. Miguel and Gina are still there, and—''

"Look, if it's the money you're worried about, don't. We can keep this thing legal until you inherit. This won't effect that."

"Dammit, Lucy, you think I'm worried about the inheritance?'' He turned her around, made her face him. "To hell with the inheritance!''

She said nothing, wouldn't even look him in the eye.

"Fine. I'll go. I'll stay in my apartment, okay? You won't even have to see me if you don't want to. I'll give you some time, if that's what you want, but, Lucy—''

"I...guess that would be okay. Just until Miguel and Gina can take the baby home from the hospital.''

He searched her face, and finally sighed, feeling utterly deflated, confused, and pretty well heartbroken. "What happened, Lucy? I thought you felt something, too.''

She refused to answer him, refused to hold his gaze. "I think you should go now. I need to get back to the hospital.''

He was so frustrated he could have screamed. "Fine. You want me to go, that's just fine."

He released her, wounded to the core, and stormed out of the house.

It seemed to Lucy very fortunate that Holden had revealed his feelings about having a child before she'd had the chance to tell him she was pregnant. It made things a lot easier. If she'd told him first, he may have tried to cover those feelings. But this way she knew where he stood from the start. And it seemed very clear to her that she had to choose—between the child she carried, and the husband who thought there might be some chance of a true love developing between them. Maybe. Someday.

She hadn't told him that she already loved him. There was no reason for him to know that. She picked up the phone and dialed the number of her old apartment. She wouldn't rush Gina and Miguel, but now that Miguel was employed by Fortune TX, Ltd., they would be finding a place of their own closer to town. Better they know that, as far as she was concerned, the sooner the better.

Holden went back to the office, but not happily. Lucy had all but told him it was over. Given him the old heave-ho before he even had a chance to get started. He wished he knew what was wrong with her.

It was noon when his secretary buzzed him to say he had a visitor. Until he heard the name, he'd forgotten all about the surprise he had planned to spring on his wife. Now, he barely knew what the hell to do about it.

"Send him in," he said with a sigh. He got up from behind his desk just as the office door opened and the man stepped through it.

He was thin, a bit too thin. His jaw and cheekbones sharply etched beneath his skin. But handsome, too. Dark skin, the large, proud nose so characteristic of Native American heritage. His hair was mostly silver, with a few streaks of raven still showing here and there. He had huge dark eyes...Lucy had those eyes.

"I'm John Brightwater," he said slowly, looking Holden up and down.

"Holden Fortune, sir." Holden extended a hand, and Lucy's father shook it, his grip firm.

The man nodded. Holden waved toward a chair. "It was good of you to come," Holden said. "Can I get you anything? A cold drink? Coffee?"

John Brightwater held up a hand, even as he took his seat. "I only want to know if it's true, what you told me on the telephone. My daughter...she married you?"

Holden blinked. "You sound surprised."

"After what you did to her? I'm surprised she would even speak to you, much less consent to be your wife."

Holden had been in the act of leaning back against the edge of his desk, but he almost fell down at those words. "You... She told you about that?"

"She didn't have to tell me. I was with her, in the hospital, when she nearly died because of what you did."

"Wait a minute, wait a minute," Holden said quickly, holding up both hands. "I don't think we're talking about the same thing here. I never did anything to hurt Lucy. Put her in a hospital? I don't know what you're—''

"Ah." John waved a dismissive hand. "I *know* it was you. She didn't tell me. I never asked, because I had no need to ask. My Lucy was a good girl. She would not have let just anyone take advantage of her. But you...I always knew she was weak where you were concerned, Fortune. She thought she loved you.'' He sniffed. "You didn't even come to see her in the hospital.''

"I didn't know she was ever in the hospital!''

John Brightwater crossed his arms over his chest and glared at Holden. Then, bit by bit, the frown lines in his face eased. A hint of doubt appeared. "It would be just like her not to tell you.''

"Then why don't you tell me? Because I'm totally lost here.''

Still scowling, eyes narrow, he finally nodded. "I don't know what happened between you and my daughter, Fortune. Only that you took advantage of her. She was an innocent.''

Holden lowered his head. "It's true. I had too much to drink one night and...hell, there's no excuse. I did it, and I'm ashamed of it. Lucy's too good to be treated that way.'' He managed to look his wife's father in the eye again. "For what it's worth, I've told her how sorry I am. And I think she's forgiven me.''

"Has she forgiven you for the loss of her child, as well, Fortune?''

"Her...'' Holden gulped in a breath.

"There was a child,'' John Brightwater said. "My grandchild. But growing inside Lucy's fallopian tube, rather than in the safety of her womb. When the child grew too large..."

"Oh, my God." Holden came off the desk, dizzy, his knees shaking. "Oh, my God, I didn't know..."

"She bled inside. The fetus had to be removed, along with an ovary. Lucy's chances of conceiving again were cut in two because of that." He lowered his head, shaking it slowly. "Perhaps less than that, given her mother's history of ovarian cancer. Perhaps I'll never know a grandchild." He looked at Holden, his gaze steady as Holden stood there, one fist clenched in his own hair. "My daughter may have forgiven you, Fortune. But I do not know that I can."

Holden sighed, dragging himself away from his thoughts long enough to feel defensive. "I wouldn't blame you if you didn't," he said. "But I swear to you, I did not know any of this. And...and besides, she could have had ten kids by now and you wouldn't have known about it. If you care so much for your daughter, Mr. Brightwater, why have you been out of her life for so long?"

This time, it was John who looked at the floor. "I failed her. So many times. I just couldn't face her anymore. I let her mother die, you know."

Holden's attitude softened immediately, along with his voice. "No, I don't know. I don't think that's true."

"It is. I knew something was wrong. I should have made her see a doctor sooner than she did. I should have—"

"No." Holden shook his head, expelling his breath all at once. "There was nothing you could have done. I'm sure of that."

"I failed her as a father, as well. If I had been doing my job, I would have protected her from men like you."

Pursing his lips, Holden decided to let that one pass. "It's history now. You can't change the past, John. Only the future. And I think your daughter needs you in her life again. That's why I sent that ticket, and asked you to come here."

John's head came up slowly, his eyes widening. "She's not sick, is she? The doctors warned us both that this cancer that killed her mother would be a risk for her. Some even suggested she have the remaining ovary removed, to prevent it."

"My God. The risk is that high?"

John looked at him steadily.

The most horrible thoughts were running through Holden's mind. What if she was sick? What if that was why she'd been so desperate to have a child that she would resort to tricking him into getting her pregnant? He should have known there was more motivating her than what she'd revealed. He should have known! No woman as good as Lucy would play those kinds of games without a damn good reason.

"I would like to see my daughter now. Perhaps it is not too late."

"It's not. I promise you, it's not." He glanced at his watch. "She'll be at the hospital, just about to take a lunch break, I think. Come on, I'll drive you there."

"No need," John began.

"Yeah, there is," Holden said. "I have some business there myself."

Fourteen

Lucy sat in her office, munching a tuna salad from the hospital cafeteria, and grimacing at the taste. The lettuce was wilted. Still, she forced it down. It was good for the baby. Her side dishes included lukewarm string beans and a carton of milk.

There was a tap on the office door. She washed her bite down with a gulp of milk, and called, "Come in."

The door opened, and the last person in the world she'd expected to see stood there.

"Dad?" She got up slowly. "My God, what are you doing here?"

He shifted his weight from one foot to the other. "I…" Then he shrugged. "I came to say that…I'm sorry. And that I love you, daughter."

The lump that came into her throat was so large, it nearly choked her. She couldn't speak. For him to show up now, of all times… She moved around the desk, went to her father, and almost cried in relief when his arms came around her.

Holden watched from across the hall, as the two embraced in the open doorway of Lucy's office. Then he nodded, and went to the next office down. He'd already checked at the nurses' desk, and there was only one other OB-GYN in residence here at Red

Rock General. Dr. Karen Flemming. So she had to be Lucy's doctor, right?

So she had to have Lucy's records.

He tapped on her office door, went in when she opened it, tried to school his face into a look of excited worry and said, "There's a lady giving birth in the parking lot! You'd better hurry!"

"Holy mother of..." was all he heard as she raced away, dragging a nurse in her wake.

As soon as she was out of sight, Holden looked both ways, and slipped into her office, closing the door behind him.

Luck was on his side. The file cabinet was unlocked. He slid it open quietly, feeling like a thief in the night as he rummaged through looking for "Brightwater, Lucinda" for a full minute before he thought to look under "Fortune, Lucinda." He closed the top drawer, and opened the next one, found the *F*s, and finally, the file he wanted.

As he pulled it out, Holden closed his eyes, and whispered a silent prayer. *Please, God, don't let me find the word cancer in here. Please...*

Footsteps came toward the door. He closed the file drawer, stuffed the file into his shirt, and took a seat, trying his best to look innocent.

The office door opened. "Dr. Flemming?" the nurse said, then scowled. "What are you doing in here?"

"Uh...waiting for my wife? Isn't this Dr. Brightwater...uh, I mean, Dr. Fortune's office?"

She had the face of a bulldog, especially when she puckered it up like that. "No. And you shouldn't be in here.'' She did a quick scan of the place, her eyes lingering on the file cabinet.

"Sorry. I just got the wrong door." Holden got to his feet.

"The name is on the door."

"Well, I, uh, forgot my glasses, as well."

"Humph," she said, and stood there, holding the door wide, waiting for him to leave. He did, and hurried toward Lucy's actual office, but he ducked around a corner before he got there.

Lucy would see to it her father was taken care of. Looked like the two of them, at least, were going to be okay. But right now, he had to get someplace where he could read through the file. Uninterrupted.

So he went back to his apartment in the city. And it was all he could do not to try to read the damned thing as he drove. But then again, he was so dreading what he would find when he pored over those pages, maybe it was better to put it off…just for a little while.

Lucy spent the entire afternoon with her father, and slowly, it seemed her oldest wounds were mending. She showed him around the hospital, then around Red Rock itself, and later took him to dinner. It helped. Focusing on her relationship with her father gave her an excuse not to think about how badly she'd screwed up her relationship with her husband. And she knew that was simple avoidance, but she needed that right now.

Dwelling on the dirty trick she'd pulled didn't do any good. She couldn't undo it. And replaying Holden's words about not wanting a child didn't do any good, either. She couldn't change the way he felt.

No more than she could change the way she felt about him.

It was hopeless. All of it. So she just wouldn't think about any of it right now.

During dinner she excused herself to make a call to Mary Ellen, who still knew nothing about the blowup between her and Holden. She didn't say anything about it, either. Just mentioned that her father was in town, and got the exact response she'd hoped for. A warm invitation. A promise he would be made to feel welcome.

As she thanked Mary Ellen and hung up the phone, Lucy thought she could easily come to love that woman. And she wondered, briefly, if Mary Ellen didn't realize it was time she find some happiness of her own, a man to love her as she deserved to be loved.

Right. And she was one to give advice in that department.

When Lucy walked her father through the front door that night, Mary Ellen was there to greet them. Clasping John's hand in hers, she said, "You must be Lucy's father. It's such a pleasure to finally meet you. I'm Mary Ellen Fortune, Holden's mother."

"John Brightwater," he said in his deep voice. "And the pleasure is mine. I told Lucy I'd be perfectly comfortable in a hotel, but—"

"Nonsense! You're family. You'll stay right here. We have so much to talk about, and this will make it much more convenient, don't you think?"

He looked slightly embarrassed by her warm welcome. Likely because he hadn't been expecting it. As Lucy recalled, her father had never had a very high opinion of the Fortune family. Maybe that would change now.

"How was your day, Lucy?" Mary Ellen asked, switching her focus. "You're feeling all right, I hope?"

"Fine. Seeing Dad was just what I needed today." She smiled up at her father as she said it, and received a loving gaze in return. "You must have a sixth sense, Dad, to show up just when I needed you."

"Nothing quite that mystical," her father replied. "It was your, uh, husband."

Lucy felt the blood drain from her face. "Holden brought you here?"

Her father nodded. "Tracked me down, and bought my plane ticket. Right now, Lucy, I have to say, I'm glad he did."

Lucy couldn't answer. That Holden would do this...reunite her with her father, in spite of everything...

"And where is Holden?" Mary Ellen asked.

That question brought Lucy up short. She didn't have an answer that would fool her mother-in-law. But she gave it a try anyway. "Um...he had a lot of work at the office. I think he said he might be staying at the apartment tonight."

Mary Ellen's smile seemed to freeze in place, but worry showed in her eyes. She shook it off, though, recovering quickly and turning as Sally, one of the maids, came into the room. "Well, Mr. Brightwater, I'm sure you'd like to freshen up. Sally, will you show Mr. Brightwater to the guest room?"

"It's John," Lucy's father said. "I'll go to the car and get my bags."

"Not necessary, John, I'll have them brought right up." She glanced at Sally, who nodded, smiled at John, and led him away. "I do hope you'll join me in an hour or so for a nightcap, John," Mary Ellen called as he left.

He nodded back at her, and then obediently followed Sally up the broad staircase.

When Mary Ellen's gaze returned to Lucy's, her smile was gone. She took Lucy by the hand and pulled her into the smaller sitting room, closing the door behind them.

"What's happened between you and my son, Lucy?" she asked.

With a sigh, Lucy sank onto the ottoman nearest her. "I don't know. Everything went wrong, Mary Ellen."

"Such as?"

Lucy swallowed hard.

"Come, Lucy, out with it. We have enough troubles in this family without adding the breakup of a brand-new marriage to the list. Did you tell him about the baby?"

"No. But I told him the truth. That I'd planned to get pregnant, and how I'd changed my mind once I saw the man he truly was."

Nodding slowly, Mary Ellen paced a few steps away. "And he was angry."

"At first, yes. But he got past it. I think he was willing to forgive me for scheming that way. But then...then he said..." Her throat swelled, and Lucy lowered her head, pressed her fingers to her lips to prevent the sob from escaping.

Mary Ellen crouched beside her instantly, hands to

Lucy's shoulders. "There. It's all right. Tell me, what did he say?"

Sniffling, Lucy lifted her head. "He said...he was glad I didn't go through with it. That he didn't...didn't want a baby...and...and—"

"Oh, Lucy." Mary Ellen's arms went around her, and she held Lucy gently as she cried. Soft, strong hands smoothing her hair. "Poor darling. That was the last thing you needed to hear."

"I don't know what to do. If he doesn't want a child, then—"

"Come now, Lucy, he didn't tell you he didn't want a child, did he?"

Taking a deep breath, Lucy shook her head. "No. He just said not now." Her eyes squeezed shut. "But, Mary Ellen, I may not get another chance. I only have one ovary, and I need to have it removed soon. And yet, I love Holden. I don't want to lose him."

Mary Ellen softened, her breath escaping her in a rush. "If you love him, Lucy, then give him a fair chance. He doesn't know the entire situation, don't you see? He doesn't know this may be your only chance to have his child. He doesn't know how desperately you want this baby. And, unless I'm mistaken, he doesn't know you love him. Does he?"

Closing her eyes again, Lucy shook her head.

"Now don't you think you should tell him all these things before you condemn him? Lucy, you've spent time with my son. You've come to see the goodness inside him just as I always have. You must know, somewhere inside you, that he would cherish this child as much as you do."

Lucy shook her head. "I don't know. I just don't know..."

"He said the wrong thing at the worst possible time for you, Lucy. But he didn't know the whole situation. Please, darling, give him another chance."

"It...would feel like I was trying to...to trap him."

"Oh, no. Lucy, Holden Fortune is not a man who would let himself be trapped. Do you know how many women have tried?"

Again, Lucy lowered her head. "Maybe..."

"Oh, for heaven's sake, daughter." Mary Ellen gripped Lucy's arms, and pulled her straight to her feet. "You are a glorious female. You are life-giving woman, in all her splendor. Now act like one. Stiffen up that spine, haul your tail over to that apartment, and fight for your man." Lucy stood a little straighter, and Mary Ellen smoothed her hair. "Fight for your baby's father, Lucy. If you truly love him, it's worth the effort. Believe me."

Slowly, Lucy nodded. "All right. All right, I—I can do this."

"You can do this."

"My father—"

"Don't you worry about your father. He and I will have a lovely visit while you're gone."

"He...doesn't know about the baby."

"And he won't, not until you and Holden announce the news to him together, side by side, just as you should be. Now go."

Brushing at her still damp eyes, but feeling suddenly empowered, Lucy nodded harder this time. "I will."

* * *

Holden couldn't believe what he was reading. But it was all here in black and white. Lucy's history. He didn't understand most of the medical terminology, but her doctors, several of them over the years, had made notations that explained it all. And one of them, dated on the day after the doomed christening party, shook him to the marrow.

"Due to the presence of precancerous cysts, and given the patient's family history, I've recommended the immediate removal of the remaining ovary. Patient extremely reluctant to consent."

"My God," Holden whispered. "My God, no wonder she so desperately wanted a baby." But why the hell hadn't she told him?

His buzzer sounded. He sent it an irritated glance and ignored it. And in spite of that, a few seconds later, someone was knocking at his apartment door.

Setting the folder aside, he went to the door and flung it open.

Becky Sue Monohan stood on the other side, cleavage spilling out of the lowcut neckline of the dress she wore, big blond Texas hair spilling over her shoulders, and legs damn near up to her neck. He'd dated her not too long ago. Looking at her, now, he couldn't see a thing that might have appealed to him then. "How the hell did you get up here? I didn't buzz you in."

She shrugged. "Someone else came in, and I just followed. I've been calling you for days, Holden," she said with a pout. "Where have you been?" As she spoke, she shouldered past him and closed the door.

"On my honeymoon." He said it clearly, quickly, leaving no room for misunderstandings. He didn't have time for this.

"Your... B-but... You got married?"

"Yes. I got married. And I'm kind of busy right now, so if you don't mind..."

"Oh, no. You're not getting rid of me that easily. If you're married, then where is your wife? Hmm?"

"At the house. Now will you please go, so I can—"

"If she's at the house, why are you here?" She looked around the place, smiled smugly. "Humph. It's one of *those* marriages, isn't it? She's cold, but socially acceptable. Not like me." She slid her palms up the front of his shirt. "It's all right, Holden. We can still—"

"No, Becky Sue, we can't. I happen to be in love with my wife."

She blinked, and stuck her lower lip out further. But seeing he wasn't going to give in, she finally turned and flounced out the door, slamming it behind her.

Sighing in relief, Holden started back for the file folder lying open on the coffee table. But then he paused, and a slow smile spread across his lips. "I love my wife," he said very softly. And it was suddenly so perfectly clear to him. He hadn't been tempted by Becky Sue in the least. He only wanted Lucy. "I'm a one-woman man. Hell, I'm *nothing* like my father."

Lucy used the keycard Holden's mother had given her to enter the building, and took the elevator up to the tenth floor. All the way, she was chanting a mental mantra. Telling herself she could do this—she could face Holden with the truth and deal with the consequences. It was her only choice, really. Mary Ellen had made her see that. She couldn't just give up everything she had without at least trying to make things right.

She could do this.

The elevator doors slid open and Lucy stepped out of them just in time to see a blond bimbo who looked like a former swimsuit model, exiting Holden's apartment.

"Oh, my God," Lucy whispered. Her heart squeezed tight in her chest and tears sprang to her eyes as the woman strode past her, not even giving her a glance as she stepped into the elevator and jabbed a button. The doors slid closed.

Lucy stood there for a full minute. She should leave. She should just leave. It was pretty clear now where Holden stood. His first night without her, and already he was...he was...

She bit her lip, and turned in search of a stairway. She didn't want to wait for the elevator's return.

A door stood at the far end of the hall with the word Stairs painted on its face in unattractive yellow block letters. But then, unbidden, Mary Ellen's voice filled Lucy's mind.

Stiffen up that spine, haul your tail over to that apartment, and fight for your man!

Clenching her teeth, Lucy turned and walked slowly to Holden's door. At the very least, she would tell him what she thought of his little tryst with the blond bombshell.

She lifted her chin, wiped at her tears with an angry hand, and knocked hard on the door.

Holden's voice, raised and impatient, came from the other side. "Dammit to hell, Becky Sue, I told you, I'm not interested!"

Lucy stood stock-still. She blinked, as her mind processed his words. He hadn't been playing around with that…that woman. Battling a small, relieved, even hopeful smile, she lifted her hand and knocked again.

"Get this through your head," Holden all but growled. The doorknob turned and the door was flung open as he said, "I am in love with my…" Then he saw her standing there. "Wife," he finished, but the word was almost a whisper.

"Hello, Holden."

"Lucy…." He pulled her into his arms, held her hard to his chest, and stroked her hair. "Lucy, God I'm so glad it's you. Baby, I'm so sorry. I didn't know. I just didn't know…."

"Didn't…didn't know what?"

She pulled away from him, searching his eyes and seeing them dampen even as she did. Then she looked past him and spotted the familiar-looking file folder lying open on the table. She gaped at him. "Holden? Are those *my* medical records?"

He lowered his head. "I'm sorry. I know it was wrong, but when your father told me what really happened all those years ago… God, Lucy, you lost an ovary—and a baby—because of me." He pulled her close again, rocking her slowly in his arms. "And now those cysts, and they want to remove the other one. Honey, if you'd told me…if you'd only told me why you were so determined to get pregnant…"

She let herself be held, comforted in his arms. All the while wondering what his motives might be now. Did he know? Did he know *everything*?

"If I'd told you…" she prompted.

He framed her face with both hands, gazing down

into her eyes. "I don't know. If the ovary has to come out, Doc, then it has to. It's your life we're talking about here. And God knows, we can adopt a baby. I don't want to risk losing you."

She tried to keep a lid on her emotions, but they were damn near swamping her. "It wouldn't be a risk to have a baby," she said. "It only takes nine months, and I could have the ovariectomy right after the birth. With close monitoring, I could have a perfectly normal pregnancy."

He searched her face. "Are...are you sure?"

She nodded.

"Then..." He took a breath, bit his lip. "Then let's do it. Let's have a baby."

She lowered her head. "I thought you said you didn't want one right now."

"That was before I knew it might be our only chance."

"My only chance, Holden. Not yours."

He stared down at her, his eyes intense and wide. "Doc, haven't you figured things out yet? Lucy, I'm in love with you. I don't want anyone else, much less a child with anyone else. Not now, not a year from now...not ever. Just you. I love you, Lucy."

She didn't reply. Just stared up at him, wanting with everything in her to believe him—to believe he wasn't just saying this because he knew she was already pregnant. "I—I just need to know one thing," she whispered, unable to speak any louder.

"What?"

Her lips trembled. She bit them to still the motion. "How much of that file did you read?"

His frown seemed perplexed. God, she hoped it was

perplexed. He glanced at the file folder. "I... About all of it, I guess." Then his face paled, and his brows rose. "Why, Lucy? Is there something I don't know. Something wrong? Did they find—"

She pressed a finger to his lips. If he'd read the entire file, then he must know she was already pregnant...and all of this was...

Then, slowly, her mind cleared. She looked again at the file. One file, and if it had all the information about her ovarian problems in it, then it had come from Karen Flemming's office.

Not Susan Martinez's.

Karen had no idea she was pregnant.

"Honey? Lucy, tell me. If something's wrong, then I—"

Lucy smiled through a new flood of tears. "Nothing's wrong. Nothing's wrong at all, Holden. In fact, for the first time, I think everything is right."

"Then what..."

"I love you, too, you know," she told him. "I always have."

He bent toward her, kissed her long and slow. When he lifted his head again, he said, "Thank God for that. Lucy, sweetheart, I do want a baby. I—the idea scared me, I admit that, but having a child with you is the most incredible gift I can imagine. And if you're sure it's safe for you..." He smiled, a sexy little smile she loved more than life. "Then I think we ought to get started right away."

"Maybe sooner than you think." He tilted his head. "Come sit with me for a minute, Holden. There really is something you ought to know."

His expression puzzled, he stepped away, taking her

hand in his and pulling her with him to the sofa. They sat, side by side, and Lucy reached for the file, flipped over the pages he'd already read, skimming them just to be sure.

"I wanted to get some birth control," she told him, closing the file at last. "But I knew my regular doctor would ask too many questions. She knew how much I wanted a child, you see. So I went to see another doctor, Susan Martinez, and she insisted on running a pregnancy test before she'd write me a prescription."

Holden looked at her, looked at the file folder again, looked back at her. "Lucy?"

"The results of that test wouldn't be in this file. I'm glad because I thought for a while there, you were only saying all these things because you knew."

"Because I knew... Does this mean...what I think it means?"

She nodded. "If you think it means you're going to be a father, then, yes, Holden. It does. I'm pregnant."

His smile was blinding, and the tear that slid from his eye to roll slowly down his cheek touched her very soul. In wonder, he laid his palm gently across her belly. Closing his eyes, he pulled her close, tenderly, gently, he held her. "I love you, Lucy Fortune. I was empty before, but you...you've filled me. You are my heart and my soul. I'll do whatever it takes to make this work. We'll build your clinic, we'll do whatever you want. Together. I swear I will make you and this baby so happy..."

"Oh, Holden," she whispered, stroking his hair. "You already have."

* * * * *

Here's a preview of next month's

*Feisty twin Vanessa Fortune
wrangles with an older man,
steely FBI Agent Devin Kincaid in*

**THE BABY PURSUIT
by Laurie Paige**

Devin Kincaid swore and cut the wheel sharply to the left as the huge red horse broke from the trees to his right. For a second, he thought the animal was a runaway, then he realized a slender figure was astride the beast.

His next impressions whipped through his mind at mach speed—that the rider was female, that she was young and lithe of frame, that her hair, lashing across her shoulders with each lunge of the stallion, was the same shade of red as the mane that tangled with her locks as she bent low over her mount's neck...and that she was racing him!

He glanced at the speedometer. Fifty miles an hour.

The primitive urge to win at all costs surged through him. He pressed the pedal downward and felt the kick of the powerful engine concealed beneath the hood of the sport utility vehicle push him against the seat.

The young woman glanced his way, then she urged the horse faster. Fifty-one. Fifty-two. Fifty-three.

The car pulled ahead, leaving horse and rider behind. A brief flare of triumph brightened the heat-laden August afternoon. It was short-lived.

Frowning, he wondered what the hell he thought he was doing, racing a kid on a horse at fifty miles per hour. If the horse had stumbled, if the girl had fallen....

Ryan Fortune would have his hide if anyone on the Fortune ranch was hurt because of him and a moment of foolishness, left over from a childhood that had forced him to fight back or die trying.

He glanced into the rearview mirror, but the horse and rider had vanished as quickly as they had appeared. Maybe he ought to tell Fortune that some ranch hand's kid was playing games with cars, probably on a prize stallion with a mile-long pedigree. On the other hand, a kid and her pranks weren't his main concern at present.

The baby kidnapping was.

With this somber thought, he parked under a tree a short distance from the ranch house, an adobe hacienda of both awesome dignity and inviting warmth. As he walked across the road toward the green sweep of lawn shaded by the oaks native to the Texas hill country, he heard the pounding of hooves on gravel and turned to face the road.

The huge red beast bore down on him. He gauged the distance between him and the rapidly approaching animal. Energy poured into him as he prepared to dive out of harm's way. Six feet away, the rider pulled up.

The beast pivoted, then rose majestically on his hind legs, front hooves pawing the air. Backlit by the afternoon sun, horse and rider blended into one dazzling portrait of fiery splendor, so bright he had to shade his eyes, so alive and fierce and powerful, he felt an answering force within himself.

The rider studied him intently, and Devin felt a visceral thrill of recognition, as if he and the unknown young woman—the woman he would come to know as Vanessa Fortune—had already met, as if this turbulent moment spoke of latent passions that had once flared between them...and would do so again.

SPECIAL EDITION

Stories of love and life, these powerful novels are tales that you can identify with—romances with "something special" added in!

Fall in love with the stories of authors such as **Nora Roberts, Diana Palmer, Ginna Gray** and many more of your special favorites—as well as wonderful new voices!

Special Edition brings you entertainment for the heart!

SILHOUETTE®

Desire®

Do you want…

Dangerously handsome heroes

Evocative, everlasting love stories

Sizzling and tantalizing sensuality

Incredibly sexy miniseries like **MAN OF THE MONTH**

Red-hot romance

Enticing entertainment that can't be beat!

You'll find all of this, and much *more* each and
every month in **SILHOUETTE DESIRE**. Don't miss these
unforgettable love stories by some of romance's hottest
authors. Silhouette Desire—where your fantasies will
always come true....

DES-GEN

If you've got the time...
We've got the
INTIMATE MOMENTS

Passion. Suspense. Desire. Drama. Enter a world that's larger than life, where men and women overcome life's greatest odds for the ultimate prize: love. Nonstop excitement is closer than you think...in Silhouette Intimate Moments!

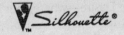

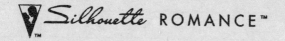

What's a single dad to do when he needs a wife by next Thursday?

Who's a confirmed bachelor to call when he finds a baby on his doorstep?

How does a plain Jane in love with her gorgeous boss get him to notice her?

From classic love stories to romantic comedies to emotional heart tuggers, **Silhouette Romance** offers six irresistible novels every month by some of your favorite authors! Such as...beloved bestsellers **Diana Palmer, Annette Broadrick, Suzanne Carey, Elizabeth August** and **Marie Ferrarella,** to name just a few—and some sure to become favorites!

Fabulous Fathers...Bundles of Joy...Miniseries... Months of blushing brides and convenient weddings... Holiday celebrations... You'll find all this and much more in **Silhouette Romance**—always emotional, always enjoyable, always about love!